THE GREENBRIER GHOST

AND OTHER STRANGE STORIES

Dennis Deitz

D1111880

MOUNTAIN MEMORIES BOOKS
Charleston, West Virginia

Mountain Memories Books
Charleston, WV

25 24 23 22 21 20 19 18 17 16 15

Printed in the United States of America

ISBN-13: 978-0-938985-08-2
ISBN-10: 0-938985-08-6

About the cover: The Historical Marker on the front cover is located on
Route 60 where it passes over I-64 at the Sam Black exit. It may be the
only historical marker in the country concerning a ghost.

Distributed by:

West Virginia Book Company
1125 Central Avenue
Charleston, WV 25302
www.wvbookco.com

DEDICATED TO MY WIFE
MADELINE
AND TO OUR 9 YEAR OLD GRANDSON ADAM GOOD WHO THREATENED TO "YELL IF THE GHOST BOOK WASN'T DONE SOON!"

ACKNOWLEDGEMENTS

Thanks to the following: Michelle Kersey, April McKinney-Warner, Christina Ferrell, Lillian Kersey and Barbara Withrow of D&M Typesetting, Inc. for their hard work typesetting, layout of *"The Greenbrier Ghost and Other Stories"*; Martha Cross Sargent and Vera Atkisson for the art work; Debbie Skidmore for typing; George Deitz, Linda Deitz Good, Charles Cornelius and Debbie Skidmore for proofreading; Max Carter for photographs; Bev Davis for the foreword; Dr. Judy P. Byers for the Introduction, editing, and tale motifing done in collaboration with her folklore students in English 371, Folk Literature, Fairmont State College, Clarksburg Campus (the name of each student responsible for motifing a specific tale appears at the end of each motifed tale).

FOREWORD

Once again, the voices of yesteryear have beckoned Dennis Deitz, and the Greenbrier County native has obligingly captured their stories in the pages of a new book.

Drawing from the narratives of more than 45 writers, the author of such popular works as *The Flood and the Blood* and *The Search for Emily* has skillfully woven their tales into a fascinating tapestry of folklore.

Deitz brings to his latest book the same homespun wit, humor, and poignance which have won him a special place among Appalachia's most treasured authors.

Roam with him now through the hollows and hills and into the hearts and imaginations of those who have shared stories of premonitions, ghosts, legends, and tales of the supernatural.

Bev Davis
Features/LifeStyles Editor
The Beckley Register-Herald

TABLE OF CONTENTS

Introduction

Dennis Deitz takes great pride in knowing a good story when he hears one. His collection of supernatural tales, **The Greenbrier Ghost and Other Strange Stories**, confirms his claim. But, of course, Mr. Deitz is a natural storyteller himself and a keen observer of his surroundings. Even though he really didn't start to write down his observations until he was seventy, now nearly a decade later, he has been more prolific than most writers in a lifetime. Spurred by his belief that "we don't have the storytellers we used to have," he has a mission "to record as much of it as possible." All of his writings, ranging from five volumes of childhood and family reflections, **Mountain Memories**, to a personalized history of the Paint Creek disaster, **The Flood and the Blood**, and a novel, **The Search for Emily**, mirror the beliefs, emotions, and heritage of his West Virginia home. His writing is imaginative and rich, steeped with the same colorful language and detail rooted at the heart of his central Appalachian culture. Through folkloric description he recreates the regional experiences of his hills and valleys.

Mr. Deitz is also a homespun folklorist as **The Greenbrier Ghost and Other Strange Stories** attests. Through his travels around the state, as a West Virginia book distributor, observing and writing, he has periodically heard strange stories that he has instinctively known he does not want to recreate, but just record as close to the actual storytellers' versions as possible[1]. Here Mr. Deitz has stepped beyond the realm of author into that of folklorist. These "strange stories", as he labels them, contain similar traits. They are not created through the storytellers' imaginations, but believed by the storytellers to be true. Usually, they are encounters that the storytellers have actually had with ghosts or other supernatural phenomena. The stories are direct, simplistic in structure, and localized in setting. A variety of his stories have been told to him by friends and family, including his wife, Madeline, and daughter, Linda Deitz Good.

When Mr. Deitz informed me last Spring of his unusual collection of stories, I was immediately intrigued. The ghost tale has a universal appeal of frightening suspense, and most people have memories of being tantalized by such stories especially as children. The ghost tale is actually a type of Sagen, a German term for a general narrative pattern used around the world. According to Stith Thompson,

> This form of tale purports to be an account of an extraordinary happening believed to have actually happened... It may tell of an encounter with marvelous creatures which the folk still believe in - fairies, ghosts, water-spirits, the devil, and the like. And it may give what has been handed down as a memory... It will be observed that they are nearly always simple in structure, usually containing but a single narrative motif (**The Folktale,** 8-9).

The supernatural sagens, more typically called the ghost tales, are prevalent in West Virginia folk literature. My mentor, Dr. Ruth Ann Musick, eminent West Virginia folklorist, specialized in this type of folktale in three published collections.[2] Plus, several volumes of ghost tales remain in her unpublished estate to be edited and published. Dr. Musick believed that West Virginia contained the right ingredients to perpetuate these supernatural tales. Its rugged and varied topography of deep valleys, ridges, and dense woods filled with shadows and patchy valley fog oozing up from the river beds to hang on the hill sides and hover along lonely, twisty valley roads set the atmosphere for the haunted. Many mountain children have witnessed the fog dancing on early wintry morns or whirling in autumn dusks. Could it be a will'o wisp or maybe an apparition of the old widow woman who died alone in her cabin up the hollow...?

Dr. Musick also felt that West Virginia has

more than a ghostly climate and geography. Many violent deaths, murders, and unusual circumstances echo from the state's history: Indian troubles, cruel slave owners, the Civil War, railroad killings, mining disasters, forest fires, wandering peddlers, and domestic violence to name a few. Such sensational events are often talked about and transmitted from one group to another, one generation to another, down through the years, preserved in the oral tradition. "The Greenbrier Ghost Story" which Mr. Deitz uses as his lead tale is based on the actual murder of a young wife committed by her blacksmitty husband. A roadside marker on Route 60 where it passes over I-64 at the Sam Black Exit commemorates the event by testifying that a ghost convicted a man of murder. Actually, Dr. Musick had collected a variant of this tale in 1967, called it "The Shue Mystery," and published it in **Coffin Hollow and Other Ghost Tales** ten years later. Mr. Deitz and his cousin, George, however, who grew up in Greenbrier County on the Nicholas County line and heard the story in the family all their lives have more complete versions in this collection.

Like a seasoned folklorist, Mr. Deitz is also highly sensitive to feature the storyteller as an intricate part of each story. The stories have been actually written down by the storytellers, many of whom are primary informants presenting their encounters or experiences with the supernatural. The individual language, expression, and style of each contributor have been retained. Often Mr. Deitz has added photographs of the storytellers plus a biographical introduction to personalize each story. One story, "The Old Haunted House," has a photograph of the Dorothy Nicholas haunted house on the opposite page. Another story, "Bicycle Wreck," is printed in the actual handwriting of ten year old Jason Hill who gave it to Mr. Deitz in that form. Typically, folklorists collect ghost tales from secondary informants, storytellers who have simply heard stories intriguing enough "to pass on" orally. Some of Mr.

Deitz's tale are, indeed, secondary in nature, but since the majority of them have been recounted by primary informants, his collection is unique. Mr. Deitz's warm unassuming manner has encouraged storytellers to relate their unusual experiences with the supernatural. Often, more than one story is woven together, such as the five premonitions by Bud Burka, entitled "Other Little Incidents" and "Pat McDonald's Story" which are really five premonition narratives, four of which were actually experienced by Pat McDonald.

One of the finest storytellers featured in this collection is Opal Haynes Anderson who contributed "Jerry's Vision and Other Strange Events." Her stories are marvelously "told on paper," a motley group of strange encounters ranging from poltergeist, witch, and devil tales to even signs of impending disaster. Collectively, they illustrate the vast range and knowledge of this exciting storyteller. She and Mr. Deitz grew up near each other, and he considers her tales to be "almost like family stories."

In addition to the splendid storytelling, the rich assortments of supernatural qualities contained in these stories are tantalizing. A dominant spiritual element permeates the tales' settings from the Civil War in "The Haunted Rock," a localized history in "The Lost Ladies of Sunrise," and the smallpox epidemic of 1903 in "A Ball of Light," to World War II, Vietnam, and even UFO's in "Grandma's Story." Most of the tales fall into one of three major types of ghosts (the helpful, benevolent spirit; the revengeful spirit; or the poltergeist) while some others are variants and extensions of the supernatural, such as premonitions and mediums. My folk literature students and I were delighted to "take on" the project of analyzing "the dead" by tale typing and motifing each story using as our major guide Stith Thompson's **Motif - Index of Folk Literature**.

Of the three types of ghosts, the revengeful spirit is the least prominent in storytelling. Could it be that ghosts being above the natural as supernatural are not usually associated with dark, sinister circumstances unless they return seeking honest justice for a bad deed? Most ghost tale collections sparsely contain examples of the revengeful ghost as is true of two of Dr. Musick's collections (**The Telltale Lilac Bush** and **Coffin Hollow**), both of which feature a revengeful ghost tale as the title story. **The Greenbrier Ghost** contains only three revengeful ghosts tales, and in each instead of fearing the ghost, the reader sympathizes with its sad plight to seek justice. In the title story "The Greenbrier Ghost" Zona Heaster haunts her mother to seek justice for her murder. In "The Ashton Ghost" Marietta comes back from the dead to find out who killed her father. Plus, in an interesting twist in "The Actress," the Wilson girl haunts Murphy Jones, her murderer. Both Zona Heaster and the Wilson girl are successful in bringing their murderers to justice, but in "The Ashton Ghost" poor Marietta remains unrevenged.

Goodness surrounds the helpful spirit that returns to aid the living. This type of ghost is often more prevalent in the oral tradition than the revengeful type. Could it be that since people find such comfort in believing in supernatural intervention, tales about benevolent spirits are easily perpetuated? In both "The Lady Who Loved Cats" and "Poppie's Ghost" the dead return to aid the living whether it be an animal ghost that feeds starving cats or a father's spirit who finds a long lost doll for his daughter.

The benevolent spirits may even be equated to guardian angels as storyteller Bob Jacobus, Master of Theology, attests in "Ghosts at Brigadoon." These guardian angels are often light bearers or messengers, coming as strangers to help those in distress. Peggy Miller's second account under "Connie and the Ouija Board" can be easily titled "The Messenger" since a stranger answers a mother's prayer to summons her husband home quickly from a logging camp because his brother has died. In my family story of "An Old Man of the Mountains," a stranger answers a lost hunter's prayer and leads him to safety. This stranger

holds a lighted lantern as does the stranger in
Betty Lusher's story "The Lighted Lantern" who
comes to save Lillian from typhoid fever. Who is
the stranger? Betty Lusher says he reveals himself
by quoting from Hebrews 13: 1-2: "Be not forgetful
to entertain strangers; for thereby some have
entertained angels unawares." The benevolent
spirit encounters are my favorite stories. I still
carry the holy card given to me at my First
Communion. The front side shows a child kneeling
in prayer in a wooded area. Hovering above is a
soft glow encircling an angel in pink and ivory
light. On the backside is the prayer to our guardian
angel:

Angel of God my guardian dear,

To Whom God's love entrusts you here.

Ever this day be at my side,

To light and guard

To rule and guide.

The most common type of spirit is the
poltergeist and this collection, as typical of most,
contains many examples. Poltergeist is a German
term, meaning "ornery spirit,' and it may reveal
various characteristics as identified in different
motifs. All poltergeists, however, have one
commonality: they are "unlaid" (unrested) spirits
of those who have died before their time, suddenly
or tragically. They float along the earth usually
attaching themselves to familiar persons or
places, thus forming the genesis for haunted
houses. Several tales deal directly with haunted
houses, as announced in their titles, for example
"A Ghost in the House" and "Old Haunted
House." The poltergeist can come in different
forms, ranging from a ten year old spook in "My
Personal Spook," a ghostly cat and dog who will
not give up the house in "Our Friends," a pinkish
lady in "The Ghost of Shelton College," and the
spirits of teenagers who have been killed in a
wreck in "April Dawn Persinger's Story."

Often poltergeists will make their presence

known in ornery or playfully annoying ways, such as haunting the exact spot of their untimely death like the spirit of father-in-law "Papaw" who haunts the couch where he was shot by a lady friend ("The Ghostly Couch") or the spirit of Grandpa Bias who after dying from smallpox at the 'Pest House' during the 1903 epidemic made its way as a ball of light back to its home to haunt a rocking chair ("A Ball of Light"). "The Haunted House of Sybene" contains a classic scenario of noises, sounds of footsteps, and doors opening. Poltergeists can even adapt to historical events, such as the Civil War setting in "The Haunted Rock" where the spirit revels in sounds of a harmonica and Dixie being sung.

Poltergeists in their spooky pranks are really harmless, and most of the informants are either intrigued or annoyed by their shenanigans. Usually when poltergeists are acknowledged publicly and widely, they are finally "laid" or rested and simply disappear as in "The Little Spook." In "The Don Page Family and Their Fun Loving House Ghost Guest Homer" Homer's restlessness led it to leave Dr. Meggie's and follow the Page family home. It stayed for seven years, seven months, and seven days performing childish pranks on the family that accepted it as one of the family. One day, out of the blue, Homer left in a VW. In "The Mystery of the Weeping Willow Tree" Grandpa puts the poltergeist to rest by burying the box of toys and aprons he had found in the attic. The tale ends with a mythological twist: a weeping willow tree grows out of the box.

One of the richest sections of **The Greenbrier Ghost** contains poltergeist tales about the West Virginia Turnpike. Basically, all of the storytellers are primary informants who have either worked on the Turnpike or patrolled its 88 miles. Interestingly enough, Mr. Deitz's own daughter, Linda Deitz Good, includes her ghostly encounters while working at the Turnpike Administration Building several years ago. Mr. Deitz in his discussion, "The West Virginia Turnpike Ghosts," questions if the hauntings were triggered by the vast areas that were disturbed in building the four lane in 1954. Farms, creeks, and especially cemeteries were uprooted. Before the road system, this whole area had been stained with various natural disasters, mine explosions, and floods. Almost all of the hauntings, however, that Mr. Deitz collected occurred between the 1954 initial building to its renovation to meet Interstate standards twenty years later. The hauntings are typical of poltergeists with an interesting variant on the vanishing hitchhiking ghost motif (that has been analyzed by Jan Harold Brunvand in his **The Vanishing Hitchhiker: American Urban Legends and Their Meanings**).

Yes, Mr. Deitz's collection of ghostly and strange tales contain enough variety and suspense to intrigue anyone looking for a "good story." But, are they true? Well, the primary informants seem to think so. And, anyway, I tend to subscribe to the late Dr. Patrick Gainer's (West Virginia Folklorist) attitude that "it's more fun to believe!" I predict Dennis Deitz's **The Greenbrier Ghost and Other Strange Stories** will become a beloved West Virginia folk tale collection for years to come.

NOTES

[1] This was particularly true while he was researching background information for his   last book, **The Flood and the Blood**, and inadvertently heard many ghost tales.

[2] **The Telltale Lilac Bush and Other West Virginia Ghost Tales** (University Press of ˙   Kentucky, 1965); **Coffin Hollow and Other Ghost Tales** (University Press of   Kentucky, 1977); **Green Hills of Magic: West Virginia Folktales From Europe**   (University Press of Kentucky and McClain Printing of Parsons, West Virginia,   1989).

Dr. Judy Prozzillo Byers
Associate Professor
English and Folklore
Fairmont State College
Folklore Executrix of Ruth Ann Musick Estate
1991

GREENBRIER GHOST

THE TRUE STORY OF THE GREENBRIER GHOST

by Dennis Deitz

I grew up about fifteen miles from Rainelle, West Virginia, the site of possibly the most noted ghost story in the United States. The story concerned the murder of Zona (Heaster) Shue in Greenbrier County and the conviction of her husband, Edward Shue, of her murder due to the evidence presented by her mother who had had visits from the grave by her daughter.

In 1886, G.S. McKeever was a student at Leonard School, at Spring Creek. During the school year 1886-87, he had an experience involving Edward Shue that would have a profound effect on a number of lives.

According to McKeever, at this time, Shue and his first wife were living in a cabin on Rock Camp Run, a tributary of Spring Creek, and on land belonging to Jim Cutlip, his first wife's father.

"Shue was a young man of rather fine physique, apparently of great strength. He had a good singing voice and seemed to take a great delight in singing sacred music. I do not know whether he was connected with any branch of the Christian church. He was a great boaster of his strength; in fact, playing the role of a bully whenever you saw him. Every few days the news could be circulated in the community that Shue had whipped his wife again. This went on for some time. I do not recall who first suggested it, but it was agreed upon among (my schoolmates) that we would go to his house some night and give him an ice cold bath in a deep hole of water a short distance from his house.

"The mob that gathered was made up of W.M. Walton, the teacher; Jim Walton, Doc Brown, Amos Williams, Jack Hannah, Doak B. Rapp and several others and myself. In casting lots, it fell on

2

Doak Rapp, Jack Hannah and myself to do the bathing. Doak volunteered to call Shue to the door and catch him.

"There are some moments that live in your mind forever and this was such a moment. There was the deathlike silence of the winter night and the biting, stinging, frost-laden air in our faces. The snow cracked and crumbled under our feet as we silently approached Shue's cabin.

"When we reached the cabin, Hannah and I concealed ourselves behind a rock bench just in front of the porch, and Doak stopped at the edge of the porch and called out. Shue came to the door in his night clothes, consisting of a shirt.

"Doak asked, 'Can you show me the way to Nathan McMillan's?'

"Shue replied with the question, 'What is your name?'

"Doak: 'My name is Raymond.'

"Shue: 'Where do you live?'

"Doak: 'I live near Alderson.'

"Shue: 'I believe I know you.'

"All this time Doak had been working a little closer to Shue and finally jumped in and caught Shue around the waist. Hannah and I went to Doak's aid and pounced on Shue like wildcats on a rabbit, but before we got there, Shue had succeeded in pulling Doak into the house and had a firm grip on the door facing with his left hand. Hannah and I seized him and the three of us gave a surge. The door facing flew off and Shue fell into our arms as limp as a rag. He never made another struggle but begged for mercy like a child.

We took him down to the water hole, broke through the ice and soused him. Then we told him why we did it. The other members of the mob stood by, not far away, and looked on.

The next day Shue went before Squire Scott at Rennick Valley and swore out a warrant for Doak, Brown, Hannah and myself. Hannah decided to change his boarding place. The warrant was placed in the hands of constable Billy Mike Gillian, who served it on Brown and me. When the state had presented its case, Brown took the stand and testified he was not at Jim Cutlip's place that night and proved it by three of the mob. These statements were all true but they were not called upon to state how close to the Cutlip place they had been. Brown was released by the court, and on a motion made by M. W. Walton, the warrants were set aside."

After this trial Shue's young wife went back to her father's home. Soon after this Shue was sentenced by the Pocahontas Court to the Penitentiary for stealing a horse. While he was in the pen, his wife got a divorce and prepared herself as a teacher and taught until she married Tinker McMillan. They reared a large family of intelligent boys and girls.

When Shue returned from prison, it was not long until he married again and set up housekeeping on the top of Droop Mountain, where his (second and third) wives died under peculiar and suspicious circumstances. He then married the woman for whose murder he was tried and convicted by the circuit court at Lewisburg.

McKeever does believe that the bathing of Shue had a consolation, in that he has felt "for a time, long time that the three school boys, totally ignorant of the fact that they were violating the law, took Trout Shue from his house one winter night when the thermometer was registering ten degrees below zero, broke the ice and performed the rites of baptism, immersing him in a deep hole of water, prolonged a good woman's life for many years."

In 1896, the Reverend R. R. Little, a Methodist circuit preacher in Greenbrier and Pocahontas counties, was called to the home of Edward Shue on Droop Mountain to officiate a marriage.

According to Reverend Little, "I arrived there some time in the afternoon of the day appointed for the wedding. The bride-to-be, a mere slip of a girl, was at the Shue home but Edward...had gone for the marriage license. I waited there patiently until far into the night. An atmosphere of tension or uneasiness seemed to embrace all of those present and would not let go. Around midnight Shue came with the license. Preparations were made for a marriage ceremony. The license was passed to me. On examination I found the license was issued in Greenbrier County and the Shue home being in Pocahontas County, I told the contracting parties I could not perform a marriage ceremony in Pocahontas County on a license issued in Greenbrier.

"Shue soon reminded me that it was a moonlight night and that less than a mile would put us across the county line into Greenbrier. So the bride and groom to be, wedding guests, and I proceeded down the country road until we crossed into Greenbrier County to the Schusler place, on the side of Droop Mountain, where I arranged to perform the marriage. When I came to the part of the ceremony where it says, if any one has any objections, speak now or forever hold your peace, I waited, and after some time I said "I object." I told him for the reason that the girl he wished to marry was a mere child. None of her people are present. It is now one o'clock in the morning and we are all here in the country road. A marriage ceremony is a sacred rite and should at least be performed under ordinary circumstances. I cannot help but think there is something not right in this case and I will go no farther. So there will be no wedding so as far as I am concerned.

"I later understood that the girl was only fifteen years old, that Shue had persuaded her to visit her uncle on Droop Mountain and when he got her away from her parents, had prevailed upon her to marry him, and that they were married in Frankfort the next morning after I had refused to perform the ceremony."

Zona Heaster was a young, beautiful girl when she married Edward Shue, and she died mysteriously two months after that marriage. Zona's mother, Mary Heaster, suspected that her daughter's death was not a natural one, and her suspicions were based on three things: first, the bad reputation of the husband; second, his two previous wives had died violent deaths by strange accidents; third, he had served time in prison for stealing a horse.

Mary Heaster began to pray that her daughter would appear to her and tell her the true story of her death. After a period of time Mary related to those about her that her daughter had indeed appeared at her bedside four times and had told her that her husband had come home from work as a blacksmith, and, in a fit of rage, had broken her neck with his strong blacksmith hands.

Mary Heaster convinced her brother-in-law to help her demand an autopsy. They went to the sheriff of Greenbrier County, who, although skeptical, was finally persuaded to order the grave opened and an autopsy performed, going by the minute details which she said she had been given by her daughter who had returned from her grave to talk with her. These details she could not have known firsthand.

The autopsy showed that Zona Heaster Shue's neck was indeed broken as described. The story spread like wildfire! The deaths of Shue's two previous wives came out. Edward Shue was arrested and tried, and the testimony of Mary Heaster was allowed in court by the defense lawyer because he thought it would be treated as ridiculous. However, her testimony, along with the wealth of circumstantial evidence, was convincing, and Edward Shue was sentenced to prison for life, where he died eight years later.

Mary Heaster's daughter now lies in her grave in the cemetery of Soule Chapel Church in a peaceful, rural area of Greenbrier County, and above her grave now stands a monument which reads:

In Memory of Zona Heaster Shue
Greenbrier Ghost
1876-1897

The same brick courthouse where Edward Shue stood trial for murder is standing today, and the records of the murder trial are still there. The words of "The Greenbrier Ghost" are recorded through the testimony of her mother, Mary Heaster.

Did those words actually come from beyond the grave? Twelve serious, solid citizens, after much deliberation, decided that they did. With this decision came the legend of the "The Greenbrier Ghost," possibly the most notable ghost story that has persisted through the years in the United States. According to **Case's Comment**, a national lawyers' magazine, this is the only case in the United States where a man has been convicted of murder on the testimony of a ghost.

George Deitz

A GREENBRIER GHOST STORY
George Deitz Collection

The purpose of this recording is so the story may go down in history to all the future generations of the family of Mrs. Betty Deitz, to whom the victim of the murder case was a first cousin. The narration of this story is by J. George Deitz, son of Mrs. Deitz, before mentioned. This story was taken from the records of the Greenbrier County Courthouse, West Virginia, written and published by the Greenbrier Dispatch, June 2, 1944. Out of the dim past, from the aged and famed newspaper file, we resurrect the story of the famous murder trial which was held in Greenbrier County forty-seven years ago. The story has been told and retold. We have had several requests from readers to reproduce it. Here it is:

"If a man die shall he live again?"

That question asked by Job puzzled humanity through the ages, never being satisfactorily answered.

We are told that our soul departs permanently at death, possibly remains inactive until the resurrection, and then goes to its appointed place.

Fortune tellers, crystal gazers, mystics and other mediums claim communication with the dead. Though they have gained many followers by means of devious, mysterious and subtle seances, none can give absolute proof of such etheral communications with the "living dead."

Possibly the most startling and corroborative evidence mediums should offer to prove their contention of conversation with the dead is the conviction of Edward S. Shue, in the Greenbrier county circuit court at Lewisburg, in 1897, for the slaying of his wife.

9

The states case against this defendant, an apparent peaceable village blacksmith of the nineties, was based entirely upon circumstantial evidence, evidence that was dreamed by Mrs. Shue's aged mother while sleeping in her rustic home, fourteen miles away from the scene of the killing, on the other side of Sewell Mountain.

Ghost stories are legend. Dreamers have come down through the centuries. But little credence is given by their visions.

When man first began to reflect upon such subjective phenomena as dreams, mania, swoons, trances and the like, the only possible explanation to them, because of limited knowledge, was that all such phenomena were due to beings like themselves, active but invisible.

What could they be but spectres, apparitions, ghosts, spiritual beings, souls?

But nobody has ever actually proved, with the possible exception of Mrs. Mary J. Heaster, mother of the slain Mrs. Shue, that the dead can come back in some form and communicate with the living.

Mrs. Heaster, beyond any semblance of doubt, is an exception. Musty records, yellow with age are on file in the ancient, historic court house at Lewisburg to prove it.

This remarkable woman, the records reveal, had four separate and distinct dreams. In each of them her daughter arose from the grave to tell and actually describe how she had been murdered. Fantastic is a poor description, but those dreams convicted Edward S. Shue of murder in the first degree.

When Mrs. Heaster first told of her dead daughter's visits, friendly neighbors and authorities slyly scoffed at the aged woman's accusations against her son-in-law. Had not a competent doctor examined Mrs. Shue when her body was found, pronouncing her dead of natural causes after all known methods of resuscitation, applied in the presence of witnesses, had failed? Surely then, this grief-stricken mother was the victim of wild and fantastic dreams induced by her shocking loss.

Mrs. Heaster steadfastly insisted her daughter's visits were not the work of her imagination; were not dreams in any sense, but actual communications.

Such beliefs and superstitions possibly were more rampant back in Mrs. Heaster's day than during the present era. It was fortunate that they were. Soon she had enlisted a number of followers to her cause.

Neighbors of the late Mrs. Shue, over on the other side of the mountain, heard the strange story and recalled unusual incidents that occurred directly after the young woman had been found dead. Dismissed as of no consequence at the time, they now loomed big, casting a shadow of doubt over the sincerity of Shue, the village blacksmith.

It was indeed true that he had acted most strangly throughout the brief period immediately following his wife's burial and preceding her burial.

He never left the head of his wife's coffin in the presence of mourning relatives or visiting neighbors, come to pay their last respects.

When the doctor rushed to the house the day Mrs. Shue had been found dead, Shue was already there holding her lifeless form tenderly in his arms.

Not once during the physician's cursory examination did he relinquish Mrs. Shue's head, holding it close to his chest while he cried in anguish and prayed that a spark of life might be resurrected in her stiffened, cold body. But Mrs. Shue was beyond all help, dead of a broken neck.

Whether or not she actually returned to this world in some manner to convict Shue of a brutal murder which had escaped detection by authorities and even her family, or whether Mrs. Heaster, in her dreams, accidentally hit upon a solution to the crime, never will be determined to the satisfaction of all.

But her dream testimony finally brought about the arrest and subsequent conviction of Shue, throwing the populace of Greenbrier county into a furor and providing one of the most interesting and unusual murder mysteries in the history of West Virginia.

Only one witness to events following the discovery of Mrs. Shue's body and later sensational trial, is still living. He is Anderson Jones, a respected Negro living at Lewisburg. Jones can vividly recall the startling events. His recitation of the fantastic mystery is given ample corroboration by court records.

Jones thinks he was about 11 years old in November, 1896, when Shue married Miss Zona Heaster, of Meadow Bluff district, at the Old Methodist church Livesay's Mill. After the wedding they took up residence in a small two-story frame building which had been the residence of the late William G. Livesay, who gave the settlement its name.

Shue, a former resident of Pocahontas county, had come to Greenbrier a short time before the wedding to work for James Crookshanks at his blacksmith shop. A towering man of unknown strength, he presented a striking figure as he forged shoes before the flaming fire. Despite his previous marriage to two wives, both of whom died suddenly, young Miss Heaster fell madly in love with Shue and after a brief courtship, they were married.

Their little home seemed one of serene happiness. No one would ever suspect it was to be darkened by tragedy.

During the first part of January, 1897, Mrs. Shue fell ill. For several weeks she was under the care of Dr. J.M. Knapp. Shue appeared very attentive to his bride's needs, giving no cause for suspicion of what was on his mind.

Early in the morning of January 22, he appeared at the cabin of "Aunt Martha" Jones, mother of Anderson, to ask if the boy could go to his house and attend some chores for Mrs. Shue. Shaking his greying head, Jones clearly recalled that Memorable day, He said:

"I can remember it well. It was Saturday. Mammy told Mr. Shue I had to go to Dr. Knapp's first and would finish some work there. He seemed to resent this, but asked if I would go later in the day."

Four times he came back to the house for me. Each time I was busy. About one o'clock in the afternoon, he came again and I agreed to run his errand. Going to the house, I felt that something was wrong. All of the doors were closed and there was an air about the place I didn't like. Reaching the steps, I saw a trail of blood. That scared me but I went to the door and knocked. No one answered. I tried it and finding it unlocked, walked into the kitchen. The trail of blood continued across the floor to the dining room. This door, too, was closed.

"Once more I knocked and getting no answer, walked in. I stumbled over Mrs. Shue's body. There she was, stretched out on the floor, looking right up at me through wide-open eyes. She seemed to be laughing."

"I was frightened but still able to reach down and shake her. She was stiff and cold. Running from the house, I called across the field to Aunt Martha: 'Mrs. Shue is dead.' As she ran to the house, I went down the road for Mr. Shue, finding him at the blacksmith shop with Charles Tapscott."

"When I told him what I had found, he let out a yell and with Mr. Tapscott started for the house. I continued on to get Dr. Knapp. When we reached the house, Shue had taken his wife from the floor, placed her on the bed and was holding her head in his arms, crying for her to come back."

"But, strangest of all, although no one thought of it at the time, he had dressed Mrs. Shue, placing one of those old-fashioned high, stiff, collars around her neck and holding it in place with some kind of scarf."

"Dr. Knapp immediately started an investigation to determine if Mrs. Shue was still alive. Throughout his efforts to revive the woman, Shue continued to hold her head, refusing to let him examine it. Finally, the doctor turned and said: 'It is an everlasting faint. Her heart has failed.' "

The next morning, Mrs. Shue's body, accompanied by her husband and several of his neighbors, was taken over the mountain to Mrs. Heaster's home. On Monday, she was buried in the little family graveyard, high upon the side of the mountain.

In the interim before the funeral, Shue never once left his dead wife's side in the presence of others. When not at the coffin, he permitted no one else to go near it, not even her mother. Taking his place at the head of the corpse, Shue guarded it closely. In addition, he placed a folded sheet on one side of his wife's head and some nondescript garments on the other. They served to keep it in an upright position.

Several days after the funeral, Mrs. Heaster was awakened from her slumber by a noise in the little cabin room. Startled, she recalled constant prayers since her daughter's death, seeking the real solution to it. Maybe they were about to be answered.

Peering through the darkened room, Mrs. Heaster made out an object. It was her daughter, dressed in the very dress she had died in. The young girl seemed about to speak but when her mother reached out her hand, seeking the coffin, the girl disappeared.

The next night, Mrs. Heaster resumed her prayers, praying long and earnestly that her daughter would return again and explain her death. Once more they were answered. Mrs. Shue was talking freely and giving her mother to understand she should be acquainted with the whole mysterious affair.

A third visit was followed by a fourth one before the murdered woman told her mother the entire circumstances surrounding her death.

Secure in the knowledge that her son-in-law was a murderer, Mrs. Heaster set out to trap him. At first it was not easy. Neighbors listened a little sadly to the story but merely shook their heads. Authorities offered little additional comfort.

Several days later, Johnson Heaster, a brother-in-law, satisfied the story had some foundation to it, went over the mountain to Livesay's Mill to talk with Shue. Their conversation further aroused his suspicions. Then after talking with Anderson Jones and others who had been present at the house when his niece's body was found, the uncle was convinced the girl was a victim of foul play.

Together, Mr. Heaster and his sister-in-law went to Lewisburg for a conference with Prosecuting Attorney, John A. Preston, one of the most brilliant lawyers of his day.

Preston had already heard of the weird story which had spread around the country like wild fire but he gave little credence to it. Now the girl's mother was before him, sincere in her efforts to trap a murderer, firm in the belief that what she had to tell was true. Her brother-in-law also was there to add his suspicions, gathered from neighbors.

For several hours, the three conversed. When they concluded the meeting, Preston started the wheels of justice moving toward one of the strangest and most fantastic murder trials ever held.

First, he questioned Dr. Knapp. The kindly old physician admitted his verdict of heart failure as the cause of Mrs. Shue's death could be wrong. She had been ailing but circumstances surrounding her death had even given him some cause for suspicion. Both men agreed an autopsy would prove whether or not Mrs. Heaster's strange theory was true. If it was not, the examination would at least serve to relieve the aching heart of a saddened mother and throw undue suspicion from the shoulders of Shue.

The next day Preston and Dr. Knapp went to Livesay's Mill, informed Shue of their plans and ordered him to accompany them over the mountain to his wife's grave. In addition, they took Aunt Martha and little Anderson. Shue vigorously protested such action but dared not to refuse to accompany the little investigating party. Throughout the long journey, he kept muttering: "I

15

don't know what in the name of God they are taking her up for. They are not going to find anything."

But he was wrong. Reaching the mountain grave, Preston ordered several neighbors to exhume the body of Mrs. Shue. Such action, although commonplace today, had never been heard of in Greenbrier county. So it was only after considerable argument and the threat of arrest that Preston succeeded in having the coffin lifted from the grave and carried up the road to the school house. Shue was taken along to the little building and required to remain in the room while Dr. Knapp performed his autopsy. First the physician looked for poison, but found no trace of it.

For three days and nights he worked over the body, seeking a cause of death. During that time Shue, visibly nervous, but maintaining his innocence, sat on a large packing box, whittling it with his knife.

Anderson Jones was there during the entire examination. On the third day, Dr. Knapp was about to give up when he made a startling discovery that had been predicted by Mrs. Heaster. Jones said:

"Dr. Knapp was working around Mrs. Shue's head. I could see Shue was getting more nervous. His whittling was not as good. Suddenly the doctor turned to Mr. Preston. They whispered together for a few minutes. Then Mr. Preston turned toward Shue and said:

"Well, Shue, we have found your wife's neck to be broken.'

Shue's head dropped. A change came over him that I can't explain, but it certainly proved his guilt to me."

Mrs. Shue's body was placed once more in the little grave, it's revenge complete. Shue was placed under arrest by Sheriff Hill Nickell. The authorities started back with him to his home at Livesay's Mill. Arriving at the house the next day, Shue seemed in brighter spirits and offered the party breakfast. When they accepted, he cooked the meal himself, then announced he was ready to go to jail.

At Lewisburg, he was charged with the murder of Mrs. Shue and placed in the county jail without bond, to await the June term of the Greenbrier circuit court for trial before Judge J. M. McWhorter.

Prosecuting Attorney Preston, and his assistant, Henry Gilmer, spent several months seeking additional evidence against Shue, both fearing the testimony from Mrs. Heaster would not convict their prisoner. In the meantime, Shue obtained Dr. William Rucker and James P. D. Gardner to defend him. Gardener was a Negro attorney, the first of his race ever to practice in the county court.

The case finally came before the court on June 30. The little court room, still used today, was taxed to capacity by neighbors from both sides of Sewell Mountain. Some came to testify, others to hear Mrs. Heaster's recital of her dreams. Little difficulty was encountered in securing a jury. Within an hour the trial was on.

In his opening argument, Attorney Preston told the jury that the state's case against Shue was entirely circumstantial but that the evidence was such as never been presented in any court before. He laid stress upon the fact the dream testimony to be presented would prove beyond doubt to be authentic and informed the jurors he could prove it.

Dr. Knapp was the first witness called. He told of conducting the post-mortem examination and finding Mrs. Shue's death had resulted from a broken neck, dislocated so perfectly it escaped his observation for three days.

At the same time, the physician pointed out that the break was of such a nature it could not have been done by Mrs. Shue in a suicide attempt. He further disclosed there was absolutely no evidence to show she had been subjected herself to any sort of violence.

The physician declared he made the usual examination when Mrs. Shue was found dead and had pronounced her demise due to heart failure only after Shue had refused to relinquish his wife's head, requesting him to make no examination of it.

Anderson Jones testified to the defendant's repeated efforts to get him to go to the house and see if his wife wanted anything. Then Jones told of finding the body.

Other witnesses stated Shue was the only person seen about or known to have been in the house that morning prior to the time his wife had been found dead. Others told how he assisted in dressing Mrs. Shue and in doing so placed a high, stiff collar around her neck. Then he added a large veil, several times folded and tied in a bow under the chin, around the collar. Still other witnesses related how the victim's head had appeared to be very loose at the neck and when not supported, dropped from side to side. Others testified that in his conversation and conduct after Mrs. Shue's death, the defendant failed to show proper appreciation of the loss he had sustained. One testified that when Shue had been summoned to the post-mortem and inquest the defendant declared he knew he would come back under arrest, but he knew they would not prove him guilty of murder.

All of this testimony was leading up to the expected dramatic appearance of Mrs. Heaster. Everything so far was purely circumstantial, and if Shue denied it, there was an equal chance of his being freed of the crime.

Never before in the history of American court had a jury been asked to convict a defendant on testimony which resulted from a dream. Attorney Preston hoped to do this and knew that despite the precedent he was setting, the jury would believe Mrs. Heaster's story as he believed it. Finally the aged mother was called to the stand.

With an air of determination, she told how she had been unsatisfied about the cause of her daughter's death and how she prayed that Mrs. Shue might return from her grave and solve the mystery. She told of the four separate visits made to her little bedroom by the daughter and how the girl described her own death at the hands of a scheming husband.

Attorney Preston knew undue elaboration on Mrs. Heaster's dreams would make them too fantastic for any jury to believe, so merely traced them lightly with his star witness. He further realized the defense attorneys would make every effort to break down the startling testimony. Then his case would be won, just as Mrs. Heaster had won him over from his own efforts to break her story down as one of vivid imagination.

Dr. Rucker, defense counsel, lost no time in getting at the dreams. Unaware of their full significance, he endeavored to blast them out of the court room as a start for his defense.

At this point, the story can be better appreciated by the testimony found in the Lewisburg court records. So important was it considered that Thomas H. Dennis, then editor of the *Greenbrier Independent* at Lewisburg, printed the entire question and answer testimony, something rarely resorted to by newspapers before the present decade. The testimony follows, the questions being asked by Dr. Rucker:

Q. "Mrs. Heaster, did you not have a dream that aroused your suspicions to lead you to have the body exhumed?"

A. "I had no dream for I was fully awake as I am this moment."

Q. "And did you not have a dream or vision that lead you to have the body disinterred?"

A. "Well, I was not satisfied that my daughter came to her death from natural causes, so I prayed that it might be revealed to me how she died. After about an hour spent in prayer, I turned over and there stood my daughter. I put my hand out to feel the coffin, but it was not there. She seemed to hesitate to speak to me, then departed. The next night, after I prayed again, the manner of her death might be shown, she appeared and talked more freely, giving me to understand that I should be acquainted with the whole matter. The third night, she returned and told me all about the difficulty, how it occurred and how it was brought about."

19

Here is what Zona Heaster told her mother:

"He came that night from the shop and seemed angry. I told him supper was ready and he then began to chide me because I had prepared no meat. I replied there was plenty, bread and butter, apple sauce, preserves and other things that made a good supper. He flew into a rage, got up and came toward me. When I raised up, he seized each side of my head with his hands and by a sudden wrench dislocated my neck."

Mrs. Heaster continued the remainder of her answer:

"Then my daughter went on to describe the home where she lived and surroundings in the neighborhood, so it was fixed in my mind as a reality. When I later described it for people living near there, they told me they could not have been more accurate themselves. And she told me I could look back of Aunt Martha Jones's in the meadow in a rocky place; that I could look in the cellar behind the loose plank and see. Her house was a square log house, hewed right up to the square, and she said for me to look at the right hand side of the door as you go in and in the right corner. Well, I saw the place exactly as she told me."

Q. "Now, Mrs. Heaster, this sad affair was particularly impressed upon your mind and there was not a moment during your waking hours that you did not dwell upon it?"

A. "No sir. And there is not yet, either."

Q. "And this was not a dream founded upon your distressed condition of mind?"

A. "No sir. It was not a dream. I was wide awake as I ever was."

Q. "Then if not a dream, or dreams, what do you call it?"

A. "I prayed to the Lord that she might come back and tell me what happened. And I prayed that she might come herself and tell on him."

Q. "Do you think you actually saw your daughter in flesh and blood?"

A. "Yes, sir, I do. I told them the very dress she was wearing when she was murdered. When she was about to leave the room, she turned her head completely around and looked at me like she wanted me to know all about it. And the very next time she came back, she told me all about it. The first time she came, she seemed as if she did not want to tell me as much as afterwards. The last night she came, she told me she had done everything she could, and I am satisfied she did all that, too."

Q. "Now, Mrs. Heaster, don't you know these visions, as you term or describe them, were nothing more or less than four dreams founded upon your distress?"

A. "No, I don't know it. The Lord sent her to me to tell it. I was the only friend she knew she could tell and put any confidence in. I was the nearest one to her. Shue gave me a ring he pretended she wanted me to have. But I don't know what dead woman he might have taken it off of. I wanted my daughter's own ring, but he would not let me have it."

Q. "Mrs. Heaster, are you positively sure there were not four dreams?"

A. "Yes, sir. They were not dreams. I do not dream when I am wide awake, to be sure. And I know I saw her right there before me."

Q. "Are you not considerably superstitious?"

A. "No, sir, I am not. I was never that way before and I am not now."

Q. "Do you believe in the Scriptures?"

A. "Yes sir, I have no reason not to believe in them."

Q. "And do you believe the Scriptures contain the word of God and his Son?"

A. "Yes, sir, I do. Don't you believe it?"

Q. "Now, I would like if I could, to get you to say these were four dreams and not visions or appearances of your daughter in the flesh and blood?"

A. "If I am going to say that, I am going to lie."

Q. "Then you insist your daughter actually appeared in flesh and blood before you on four different occasions?"

21

A. "Yes, sir."

Q. "Did she not have any other conversation with you other than upon the matter of death?

A. Yes, sir, some other little things. Some things I have forgotten, just a few words. I just wanted the particulars about her death, and I got them."

Q. "When she came, did you touch her?"

A. "Yes, sir. I got up on my elbows and reached out a little farther, as I wanted to see if there was a coffin, but there was not. She was just like she was when she left this world. It was just after I had gone to bed. I wanted her to come and talk to me and she did. This was before the inquest and I told my neighbors. They said she was exactly as I told them she was."

Q. "Had you ever seen the premises where your daughter lived before these visits?"

A. "No, sir. I had not. But I found them exactly like she told me they were. And never laid eyes on them until after her death. She told me all of this before I knew anything about the buildings at all."

Q. "How long was it after you had those interviews with your daughter until you did see the buildings?"

A. "It must have been a month or more after the examination."

Q. "You said your daughter told you that down by the fence in a rocky place, you would find something?"

A. "She said for me to look there, but she didn't say I would find anything, just for me to look there."

Q. "Did she tell you what to look for?"

A. "No, sir, she did not. I was so glad to see her I forgot to ask."

Q. "Have you examined the place since?"

A. "Yes, sir. We looked at the fence a little but didn't find anything."

Shue spent nearly an entire day on the witness stand seeking to build a defense for himself. He talked at great length and was very minute and particular in describing unimportant events, but denied practically every thing testified by other witnesses. He entered a positive denial of the charges against him, terming the prosecution spite work. In closing he vehemently protested his innocence, calling on God to witness. Though admitting he had served a term in the penitentiary, he declared he loved his late wife dearly, and appealed to the members of the jury to look into his eyes and then say if he was guilty.

But this man's testimony and his desperate efforts personally to sway the jury made a most unfavorable impression. So great did the state's case appear against him that Dennis, editor of the Greenbrier Independent said in his paper:

"There is no middle ground for the jury to take. The verdict inevitably must be for murder in the first degree or for an acquittal."

The body solemnly filed from the room to perform their duty, returning in an hour with a verdict of murder in the first degree, but recommended life imprisonment.

After the verdict had been announced, Mr. Dennis again wrote in his paper:

"Taking the verdict of the jury as ascertaining the truth, we must conclude that Shue deliberately broke his wife's neck - probably with his big, strong hands - with no other motive than to be rid of her so that he might get another one more to his liking."

The twelve man jury and men spectators in the courtroom did not see eye to eye in regards to a proper verdict. Many persons not connected with the trial expressing the opinion that the death penalty should have been imposed. Rumors of mob violence grew. Sentiment crystalized. On the Sunday following Shue's conviction, a small mob gathered at Meadow Bluff camp grounds for the purpose of taking the prisoner from his cell in the county jail and hanging him. Shue's fate, the mob decreed, should be the same he had judged and carried out for his innocent wife - death by a broken neck.

At ten o'clock, they gathered at their rendezvous, eight miles from Lewisburg. One man, however, decided his neighbors were making a terrible mistake. He was George M. Harrah. Harrah, hearing of the plan, mounted his horse and hurried to the house of Sheriff Nickell at Meadow Bluff. Both men started for Lewisburg to protect the prisoner, but to reach there, had to pass the camp grounds.

Somebody in the mob recognized the sheriff as he sped down the road past the grounds on his horse. Several would-be lynchers gave chase, finally capturing the two men at the point of pistols. Sheriff Nickell drew his gun and was about to fire, despite overwhelming odds, when he recognized his assailant. Desiring not to kill the gunman, even at the cost of his own life, the sheriff tried moral persuasion.

Mob leaders went with him to the nearby home of D.A. Dwyer. There, after considerable argument, Sheriff Nickell won his point. The mob disbanded, giving him the new, stout rope with which they had planned to carry out the hanging of Shue.

Two days elapsed before Shue was removed to the Moundsville Penitentiary, to serve the remainder of his life. He died there eight years later.

THE UNLAWFUL BAPTISM OF EDWARD SHUE

As told by G.S. McKeever

Some weeks ago, I read in the Greenbrier Independent, a complete account of the trial and conviction of Edward S. Shue for the murder of his wife near Lewisburg in 1896. Having some previous experience with Shue, I have been requested by the editor of that paper and a number of other people to write it for publication. However, before giving my own personal experience, I will preface it by relating the following experience of the Reverend R.R. Little, a Methodist preacher, then in charge of a circuit composed of a number of appointments in the Greenbrier and Pocahontas counties. Reverend Little's story as related to me in person at the time of the Shue trial in Lewisburg is as follows:

"I was called to the Shue home on top of Droop Mountain, to perform a marriage ceremony. I arrived there sometime in the afternoon of the day appointed for the wedding. The bride-to-be, a mere slip of a girl, was at the Shue home. Edward (Trout) Shue had gone for the marriage license. I waited there patiently until far into the night. An atmosphere of tension or uneasiness seemed to embrace all of those present and would not let go. Around midnight, Shue came with the license. Preparations were made for a marriage ceremony. The license was issued in Greenbrier County and the Shue home being in Pocahontas County, I told the contracting parties I could not perform a marriage ceremony in Pocahontas County on a license issued in Greenbrier."

"Shue soon reminded me that it was a moonlight night and less than a mile would put us across the county line into Greenbrier. So the bride and groom to be, the wedding guests and I proceeded down the country road until we crossed into Greenbrier County to the Schusler place, on the side of Droop Mountain, where I arranged them to perform the marriage. When I came to the part of the ceremony where it says, "If any one has any objection, speak now or forever hold your peace," I waited, and after some time, I said, "I object." Shue at once demanded to know why I objected. I told him for the reason that the girl he wished to marry was a mere child. "None of her people are present. It is now one o'clock in the morning and we are all here in the country road. A marriage ceremony is a sacred rite and should at least be performed under ordinary circumstances. I cannot help but think there is something not right in this case and I will go no farther. So there will be no wedding so far as I am concerned."

"I later understood that the girl was only fifteen years old, that Shue had persuaded her to visit her uncle on Droop Mountain and when he got her away from her parents, he prevailed upon her to marry him, and that they were married in Frankfurt the next morning after I had refused to perform the ceremony."

During the year 1886-87, M. W. Walton taught school at Leonard, at Spring Creek. In addition to those people who rightly belonged to this school, there were about eighteen lads from the surrounding community also attending the school. At this time, Shue and his first wife were living in a cabin on Rock Camp Run, a tributary of Spring Creek, and on land belonging to Jim Cutlip, his first wife's father.

He, a young man of rather fine physique, apparently took great delight in singing sacred music. I do not know whether he was connected with any branch of the Christian church. He was a great boaster of his strength, in fact, playing the role of a bully whenever you saw him. Every few days the news would be circulated in the community that Shue had whipped his wife again. This went on for some time. I do not recall who first suggested it, but it was agreed upon among us that we would go to this house some night and give him an ice cold bath in a deep hole of water a short distance from his house.

The mob that gathered was made up of W.M. Walton, the teacher; Jim Walton, Doc Brown, Amos Williams, Jack Hannah, Doak B. Rapp and several others and myself. In casting lots, it fell on Doak Rapp, Jack Hannah and myself to do the bathing. Doak volunteered to call Shue to the door and catch him.

There are some moments that live in your mind forever and this was such a moment. There was a deathlike silence of the winter night and the biting, stinging, frost laden air in our faces. The snow creaked and crumbled under our feet as we silently approached Shue's cabin.

When we reached the cabin, Hannah and I concealed ourselves behind a rock bench just in front of the porch, and Doak stopped at the edge of the porch and called out. Shue came to the door in his night clothes, consisting of a shirt.

Doak asked, "Can you show me the way to Nathan McMillan's?"

Shue replied with the question, "What is your name?"

Doak: "My name is Raymond."

Shue: "Where do you live?"

Doak: "I live near Alderson."

Shue: "I believe I know you."

All this time, Doak had been working a little closer to Shue and finally jumped in and caught Shue around the waist. Hannah and I went to Doak's aid and pounced on Shue like wildcats on a rabbit, but before we got there, Shue had succeeded in pulling Doak into the house and had a firm grip on the door facing with his left hand. Hannah and I seized him and the three of us gave a surge. The door facing flew off and Shue fell into our arms as limp as a rag. He never made another struggle but begged for mercy like a child.

We took him down to the water hole, broke through the ice and soused him. Then we told him why we did it. The other members of the mob stood by, not far away, and looked on.

The next day, Shue went before Squire Scott at

27

Rennick Valley, and swore out a warrant for Doak, Brown, Hannah, and myself. Hannah decided to change his boarding place. The warrant was placed in the hands of constable Billy Mike Gillian, who served it on Brown and me. When the state had presented its case, Brown took the stand and testified he was not on Jim Cutlip's place that night and proved it by three of the mob. These statements were all true but they were not called upon by the state how close to the Cutlip place they had been. Brown was released by the court, and on a motion made by W.M. Dalton, the warrants were set aside.

After this trial, Shue's young wife went back to her father's home. Soon after this, Shue was sentenced by the Pocahontas Court to the Penitentiary for stealing a horse. While he was in the pen, his wife got a divorce and prepared herself as a teacher and taught until she married Tinker McMillan. They reared a large family of intelligent boys and girls.

When Shue returned from prison, it was not long until he married again and set up house keeping on the top of Droop Mountain where his second wife died under peculiar and suspicious circumstances. He then married the woman for whose murder he was tried and convicted by the circuit court at Lewisburg.

This is a somewhat extended history of possibly one of the greatest criminals of this state. If there ever was such a thing as honor connected with this Shue affair, it was due to my friend, Doak D. Rapp. It was he alone of all those gallant knights, who had the courage to beard the lion in his den. Well, all of this happened fifty six years ago. Mr. Rapp has proved himself an honorable and upright citizen and I see by the paper that he is aspiring to represent Greenbrier County in the West Virginia House of Delegates.

The only consolation the writer has ever had for participating in the bathing of Shue is that he felt for a long, long time that the three school boys totally ignorant of the fact that they were violating the law, took Trout Shue from his home one winter night when the thermometer was registering ten degrees below zero, broke the ice and performed the rites of baptism, without first having been ordained, by immersing him in a deep hole of water, prolonged a good woman's life for many years.

OTHER GHOST STORIES

Janet Quillen and her dog Treve

THE GHOST OF SHELTON COLLEGE

by Janet Quillen
(Thanks to the St. Albans Community News)

When I was young, my parents made a drastic decision. It was certainly one that would have a great deal of influence on the rest of my life - they decided to move.

Well, that is not such a big deal. A lot of people move, uplifting their roots, selling their homes, taking their children to new and different surroundings.

My parents were no exception; they sold the house I had always thought of as home on College Circle. And they moved up the hill - literally up the hill into Shelton College.

* * *

I CAN'T SAY I remember clear details about that adventure, but I can remember the excitement the house gave us children. I think the one big thing I shall never forget is the thrill I felt when my father would open the door halfway up the stairs which sealed the second story.

It was in rough shape for the longest time and was strictly "off limits." But once in a while my father would open it and we would peer up the stairs and wonder what was up there. I shall never forget the strong, musty smell which would rush down the steps, adding to the awe and mystery of the hidden place. For the first several years that we lived in the house, all activities were confined to the first floor.

I can remember how cold the floors were in the morning and how we would rush to the kitchen to sit on chairs with our feet sticking in the oven. As a child, I found it great fun but now, as an adult, I marvel at what my parents must have gone through.

Because of all the renovation going on, it seemed like we were constantly being shuffled into new bedrooms. For a while we would sleep at one end of the house, then be moved to the other. At times we all slept in a main room together in dormitory fashion.

My favorite room was on the ground floor with a view of three sycamore trees and the city of St. Albans sprawling in the background. I used to lie at night when I could not sleep and make pictures out of the branches of those trees. They were nice companions when my sister would not tell me a story or sing me to sleep. But this particular room had a tale all its own and my sister and I found out about it on one of those nights when sleep was difficult.

She had been telling me a story of sorts and we were both becoming rather tired. I had tried opening the curtains and looking at my trees, but tonight the picture branches didn't work as we had tried the story approach. She had reached the end of her tale and was yawning when I happened to look toward the doorway. At the same time, my sister turned toward the door.

There in a glow of soft, pinkish light stood our mother in her usual flowing nightgown. She moved slowly to the bed, her features gently subdued by the light from the windows. She came over to us and though I am not certain, I thought she was smiling. Then my sister asked sleepily for a drink of water.

* * *

MOTHER SAID NOTHING, just continued to stand quietly, looking down at us. Again my sister asked for the glass of water and still no response. My sister and I came to the same conclusion almost simultaneously.

"Janet," my sister asked ever so timidly. "That isn't Mother, is it?"

"No," I said quietly and firmly pulled the covers over my head.

"AAAAH!" screamed my sister and joined me rapidly under the safety of blankets.

We almost went crazy when something began pulling on the covers, trying to drag us out of our safe beds. It was only when we became brave enough to open our eyes and see the lights were on, did we realize that Mother was really there.

"Girls, girls! What on earth is wrong!" she demanded.

We both looked her over carefully to make certain that this was the real Mother. And we felt no better when she tried to reassure us there was no one else in the room.

We were both quite certain of what we had seen; it was not a comforting thought. It made little difference that adults could stand there and tell us we had only seen reflections of light moving and that, combined with our active imaginations, had caused us to believe we had seen something.

We were wrong; there are no such things as ghosts. But on that particular night, my sister and I **knew** different. For us, old Shelton College would never quite be the same.

AS TIME WENT BY, other members of the family had strange things happen which seemed to lend support to our ghost sighting. There were occasions when a rocking chair would be found rocking when there was nobody around, let alone in the chair.

Or the radio would come on for no apparent reason. There was, of course, the sound of someone walking down the hallways, but we children were assured that it was merely the floorboards creaking as old houses are prone to do.

Somehow that didn't change the fact that it sounded as if **someone** was walking down the hall.

And there were other people who had actual sightings of our mysterious, ghostly encounter. Most of these were quick, out of the corner of the eye glimpses of a glowing, pinkish form moving across the hallway.

I even witnessed seeing the 'pink lady' moving at the end of the hall one night quite late several years after the sighting with my sister.

The form seemed to float across the hall and again so closely resembled my Mother that I almost called out her name. But once you have actually had a ghostly occurrence, you are never quite the same. I found there was no way I could so much as let out a squeak. (I also made it up the stairs to my bedroom in record time!)

* * *

NOW, I DON'T confess to knowing anything about the supernatural, ghosts and goblins. I only know that the ghost of Shelton College must be a relatively nice spirit for she (we are certain it is the female gender) has not carried on with such pranks and practical jokes as is the sad case with a poltergeist. (Thank goodness for that!)

Once when I was sleeping in our guest room where she has been seen most often, I felt something very cold firmly touch my arm. I was almost awake and assumed it was someone sent to summon me to dinner.

"Okay, okay, I'm awake," I mumbled. But when I opened my eyes, I was quite alone. When I later questioned everyone, no one had been down in my room. Odd, maybe coincidence, right?

My grandmother, who lived in the room for a time, once confided in my sister that she had seen this 'pink lady' in the room, but had been afraid to say anything to anyone for fear they would think she was quite out of her head.

Luckily, my grandmother, told the right sister and she was assured she was not the first person to have had such an experience.

Of course, there were drawbacks living in a "haunted house." My poor brother found that out the hard way when he decided to really scare us.

He slipped into our bedroom after the lights were out and hid under the bed. Then when the time was right, he crawled out and silently lifted his head up beside the mattress. Too bad he didn't understand what happens to the minds of two young girls when they have been so thoroughly frightened and no one believes them!

* * *

WHEN WE SPOTTED a head rising up in the darkness, this time we acted! My sister screamed out and grabbed the creature by the neck, shaking it furiously. Although younger, I was equally determined to do my share of destruction and snatching my pillow, began to slam it repeatedly over the creature's head.

It seemed very effective because the creature gasped loudly for air, but could not escape our onslaught!

That was, until the lights came on and we saw that the creature was surely no ghost, but our own brother!!

Even though we were all punished for being so ridiculous and almost killing our brother, we felt it was worth while for this time we had met our fears and had been victorious!!

As we have grown older, we have not seen as much of the ghostly lady. Or maybe it is because we have become so accustomed to her that we don't notice the strange squeaks and bumps in the night.

Ah, who knows, maybe the whole thing was just a childhood imagination runing wild, but then again...

A GHOST IN THE HOUSE

by Jessie Patterson and
Amanda Holstein

There is a ghost in my grandma's house. Her name is Mary. She died in my grandma's bedroom. My grandma laid nine dollars on the bed and then five dollars was gone. She covers my grandma up at night. "When my Aunt Debbie goes to the bathroom she hears someone talking to her but there's not a soul up. Once my grandma had a pizza already cooked and the ghost took it. She won't hurt you if you don't hurt her. My other grandma seen her in a pink dress. She stays in the attic. But of course my Uncle Rodney doesn't believe in ghosts.

Amanda Holstein and Jessica Patterson

The Dorothy Nicholas Haunted Home

THE OLD HAUNTED HOUSE

by Judith A. Grossl

No matter what you may think, I know I believe what a neighbor woman told me. Now I want to tell you her chilling tale...

After living in town for a couple of years, Bill and Jean decided they would move to the farm and renovate the old log house. There was no electricity and no plumbing. It was like a wilderness. They set to work clearing and cutting brush, and putting out the crops. The work was slow and tiresome. The old house had two large rooms downstairs and one large room upstairs. The stairway going upstairs always seemed to have an eerie feeing about it. Jean felt there was something really 'spooky' about that stairway.

One evening when they were sitting on the porch, a lady dressed in white came walking around the house and sat down on the steps. She didn't say a word and finally got up and walked back around the house. Bill and Jean followed to see where the woman went. Years before, there had been an old cellar built into the hillside for keeping fruit, milk, butter, and so on. The lady in white walked to the entrance of the abandoned cellar and vanished. Several evenings about dusk, the lady would walk around the house, sit on the steps, then retrace her path to the cellar. A cherry tree grew beside the cellar. When Bill cut the tree for firewood, the lady never appeared again.

In the fall they cut and threshed a few bushels of wheat. They put it in the big room at the top of the house to dry, so it could be later taken to the mill and ground for flour. About eight inches of wheat covered the floor. One night after retiring, Jean heard someone walking in the upstairs room. She woke Bill and told him to listen. Indeed, someone was walking from one end of the room to the other end through the wheat. It sounded like a size fifteen shoe. It walked back and forth, back and forth, crunching the wheat underfoot. Finally

Bill decided to go upstairs and see who was there. There was no electricity in the house, just oil lamps. There was a flashlight, but no batteries. Bill got his shotgun, but it had no shells. So he got the fireplace poker, and Jean, shaking like a leaf, carried a lamp. They ventured to the top of the stairs...but no one was there. Not a grain of wheat had been disturbed. Both windows in the room remained locked. No human could have gotten out of the room without coming down the stairway. Bill and Jean put out the lamp, took a lantern, and went to the barn. They got in their truck and headed for town and Bill's mother's for the night. They returned to the farm the next morning.

Everything remained quiet for several weeks; then...one night Bill and Jean awoke to the sounds of someone in the next room, prying up the flooring with a crowbar. When the lamp was lit, no one could be seen in the room. The linoleum on the floor was in no way disturbed.

About a month later, they were awakened by someone walking across the front porch. They had butchered a hog, and the hams had been hung in sacks on the front porch to cure. So they thought someone was trying to steal the hams. It was a brightly moonlit night and they could see as plain as day. They looked out the window but there was nothing or no one to be seen. Bill opened the door. The hams were right where he had left them...but the sounds of the footsteps stopped.

Bill and Jean moved back to town the next day.

BICYCLE WRECK
by Jason Hill

I was in bed and fell asleep. The next thing I knew I was riding my bike as fast as I could. Then I found myself on the ground with my foot caught in the spokes. I looked and saw a car shooting toward me. I yelled and my friend Mike Dempsey came and pulled me away just in time. Then I woke up. The next day I was riding my bike as fast as I could. I wrecked and saw my foot caught in my spokes. I saw a car. I yelled. Mike pulled me out of the way. I sat and thought and I remembered I had that dream.

4th grade
Jason Hill
age 10
Valley Elem.

Jason Hill

Mike Dempsey

OUR FRIENDS

by M.E. Huber

There's a house in our family that hosts three boarders. Three non-paying boarders. More to the point, **unseen** boarders! Call them what you will; ghosts, phantoms, spirits. Three separate discernible entities reside on the premises along with its human inhabitants.

The first known entity is that of a person. It has been around the longest. The other two are animals. Former pets, perhaps, who have returned not wishing to leave a good home. For the record, one is a cat, the other a dog.

The names have been omitted "to protect the innocent" so to say. They are all true, honest reports from children and adults alike.

The first entity, "Old Friend" we call him (gender is unknown), as I said, has been around the longest. He seems to reside in a closet in an upstairs bedroom. This closet also has the entrance to the attic.

We determined this to be his place of residence based on the reactions of the family cat. At times, the cat would be shut up in this spare bedroom while the family was out at school or work. Upon his release, this normally quiet mild mannered cat would act like a pinball, bouncing around, nervously looking about as though she were being chased. One might say, "Of course, any cat would act that way after being confined." Hyperactivity and paranoia are hardly the same. This cat was paranoid!

Old Friend was mild mannered for a ghost. He has been seen only once and that was recently and, of course, another story. When he's around you hear footsteps upstairs or coming down the stairs or walking through the dinning room into the kitchen. Yes, old houses creak but you and I know that a creak of the house settling does not have a heel-strike preceding it!

He is also rather mischievous at times. He has been known to hide homework assignments (that's a new one for your teacher) or move things from one place to another.

My favorite tale of the Old Friend is the day one of the boys of the family went in to watch TV in his parents room. He switched on the TV and stretched out on the bed to enjoy the ball game. Suddenly, he could hear someone breathing heavily beside him. He sat up. All he heard then was the game and someone's lawn mower. He stretched out again. Sure enough, the heavy breathing was still there. The boy sat up and turned and said, "If it's OK with you, I'm just going to sit here and watch the ball game."

I've spent the night in the downstairs bedroom, now used for guests, and have heard footsteps walk up to the door of the room and stop. You call out. No one there. Your heart beats faster, you take a deep breath and say, "It's only the Old Friend" and try to go back to sleep.

Two of the family's granddaughters spent the night in that same downstairs bedroom while visiting during the holidays. They both knew well the family tales of the Old Friend.

It was late and everyone else in the house was asleep. The midnight munches had hit. The girls were sequestered in their room and were reluctant to venture out into the cold dark kitchen. This had to be a joint venture, for neither of them would attempt this at night alone.

Then they heard footsteps in the kitchen. They continued around the corner and stopped at their door. The door was half open. Through the door, they saw him, the Old Friend. A whitish cloud with no features or appendages. Just a cloud. He vanished quickly. Both girls assured each other that they had indeed seen the same thing. Needless-to-say, this curbed their midnight munchy attack.

The two animal entities are recent additions. We believe that they are old family pets based on recognizable characteristics.

The dog, as in real life, doesn't make a lot of noise. We knew it was her from the shuffling gait and clicking of claws on the kitchen floor. Oh, of course the way she sighs. Occasionally, she'll saunter through the kitchen and stop at the door to the downstairs bedroom and sigh as if she is disappointed to find out that it's occupied and she is out a soft place to sleep.

That cat entity is more vocal in her appearances. (Cats are soft walkers.) She will, all of a sudden, meow in the dining room. There is no living cat in residence at this time, so...

The cat's litter box used to be kept in the upstairs bathroom (one box in the basement also) and she inevitably would want in when humanly occupied. She would meow pitifully at the door and reach her paw underneath it, begging for admittance. The owner, while on the throne, would reach over and open the door. This happened on a typical Sunday afternoon. As well trained as he was, the master of the house opened the door. He was rather taken aback when he remembered that he no longer owned a cat!

These entities are as much a part of the house and family as any piece of furniture or family member. They have brought much anxiety to those humans in residence, but never fear or harm. They have provided many a night's entertainment telling and retelling stories and anecdotes of the Old Friend, the dog and the cat. All in all, they are just considered part of the household, our friends after all.

But I'm glad they don't live here!

THE DON PAGE FAMILY AND THEIR FUN LOVING HOUSE GUEST/GHOST HOMER

by Don Page

I met the Don Page family several years ago and mentioned to them, as I did to many people that I planned to write a book on ghosts, premonitions, etc. They promised to give me their story of Homer the loud, noisy, mischievous ghost who lived with them for nearly eight years. This is the story as told by Don Page:

We've never been able to determine whether it was the ghost or a companion ghost that went from one place to another. It kind of appeared like it was two of them and then other times we thought maybe he was moving from location to location, the two locations being Union in Monroe County and Smithers in Fayette County, both of them in West Virginia.

In talking about Homer, when he became our resident ghost at Kanawha Avenue in Smithers, it appears he came with us after we had visited with Dr. Maggie Ballard in Union, West Virginia. I had been her house guest from time to time when I was in the area restoring an old mill over in Zenith.

For some reason, on Farmer's Day in June 1970, we were guests at Dr. Maggie's house and we were having tuna fish with pineapple in it, which was a new experience for us, and mint tea. At that time, it seemed that we had an extra guest with us. We just seemed to have that feeling, because there were only three or four of us there, but it felt like the house was crowded.

I had been a house guest at Dr. Maggie's before and she had told me about Homer who she had named. We would be busy at the house talking and doing things, and she would be looking for some particular item and naturally, couldn't find it, and she'd say, "Well, I can't lay my hands on that right now, Don, but it will turn up." Strange enough, things did turn up.

She'd say, "Well, there's those scissors! I came here this morning, knowing full well I'd left them there, and I checked for them, but I couldn't find the scissors, and now, will you look there? There's the scissors right here."

I said, "Yeah, they're there." She said, "That crazy Homer. He's always doing things like that to me." Well, I thought Dr. Maggie was very eccentric anyway, and we just went on, but these incidents happened a lot and she'd say, "Oh, that Homer."

When my wife and I left Dr. Maggie's that day, it was the date we figure that either Homer or Homer, Jr., his son or brother or whatever, went home with us to Smithers, West Virginia, and things began to happen at our house.

The worst thing was the noises. One time at Dr. Maggie's I was awakened about 6:30 in the morning by the loudest banging and running up the stairs and slamming of doors and the whole house shook. I was lying in bed waiting to see if she was going to stir around and get up and start our breakfast and then I'd come downstairs.

Wham, bam! Down the stairs and thump, the door slammed and the whole house shook. I said, "Good night! It must be one of her nephews who dropped paperwork in for her to do," since she kept the books for their trucking company.

So at breakfast I said, "Well, it seemed that your nephews were really in a hurry this morning." She replied, "They haven't been here." "What? Well, who was here this morning?" I questioned. "What do you mean?" she asked. I said, "I never heard such a racket on the stairs and I thought they were going to tear the doors off the hinges when they slammed them."

"That Homer," she said, "he's upset about something." "What are you talking about? Nobody here?" I asked. Her reply was, "There hasn't been anybody here, and those boys haven't been by here. He's done that before. He's just upset." "Do you reckon it's because I'm here?" I asked.

"You never know with Homer," she said. But I swear to you, I have never heard so much noise. I was full awake at 6:30 - and I'm telling you that whole house shook.

Well, that was typical of Homer. He was a real racket maker and when he came home with us to Smithers, our stairs became his favorite stomping ground. Up and down those stairs he would go, and I would accuse the children. We had teenagers at the time and they were always going up and down the stairs. But when I checked, they'd either be out playing or not even be home.

Then I had a younger one that would have house guests and the kids, we'd send them up to bed, and I am telling you, it would be about midnight and my wife and I would be watching television or something, and I'd say, "I'm going up there and I'm going to whip those children. They're tearing the house down." It was like they were turning over dressers and rolling a bowling ball across the floor or something. You never heard such a racket. I couldn't even hear television. I'd get up to go upstairs and my wife would say, "I just came from upstairs a while ago, honey. You were watching TV. I checked the children and they were sound asleep. They're not doing anything. That's just Homer."

We could just list on and on the number of things that Homer liked to do, but what Homer liked to do was just cause excitement. He brought excitement to our lives. He liked to be around young people, evidently, and the kids would just laugh at us when we'd accuse them of things, because they hadn't done them. He gave us something to talk

48

about. We'd tell people about the crazy things that went on at our house.

I was one for safety, and we'd find things on the stairs. I had instructed my children and told them that they weren't to leave things on the stairs. I'd fuss at my wife. "Someone's going to get killed, going to fall down these stairs." The craziest things would appear on the stairs. There's no reason that anybody would want to carry those things - gardening tools, dishes, picture frames -and put them on the stairs, things nobody would have reason to leave on the stairs.

I'd find them and I'd fuss at the family for leaving them on there, and no one ever left the things on the stairs. They did not do it. We were quite an honest family. We didn't lie to each other, and we fessed up to things, but those things were always on the stairs, and I think what Homer liked was just getting people in trouble.

We learned to sleep with him doing the crazy things he would do. It didn't seem to bother us, but people thought we were nuts when we would tell them about it. Sometimes it would get us concerned because we wouldn't know what was happening in the other part of the house, and we were the kind of people who didn't lock our doors. You didn't have to in Smithers. We would think that somebody would come in, but we would be upstairs, and if such things were happening, we'd think, "Well, maybe they're tearing up the whole house or we've got vandals or whatever," but no one was ever there.

This would go on, so there was always excitement at our house. He was a fun ghost, and maybe he helped see us through some sad times, because the things he did were just nuisance things. My wife would wake up when he would click a switch on, and we'd just jump and be startled.

There was a switch in our downstairs bathroom that was extremely loud. Ours was an old house and the noise seemed to travel in it. You'd turn that light on and, click, it would go, and it would wake us up. It got to be that some nights we'd hear, click, click, click, click, click, click, click, click! We'd walk to the head of the stairs and the bathroom light was flashing on and off. Well, my wife got upset with it because it would wake her up and make her nervous, but Homer wouldn't quit.

She said, "Honey, isn't there one of those silent light switches you can get?" I was a contractor, and I said, "Yes, there's a mercury switch. It doesn't make any sound." I put it on there and it didn't make a sound, so the light would keep flashing a few nights at different times, but it wouldn't make the click and it didn't cause us any problems, so Homer quit. He didn't do that any more, but he did flash it on a few nights at different times, but since it didn't startle us and didn't worry us, he didn't do it any more.

One night, my wife and I were lying in bed and having pillow talk, you know, as you do, talking about some things. Remember, Homer was a stair ghost. He'd come up those stairs, and he would take a couple of steps and stop. I heard this creak, creak, and a stop, and a creak, creak, creak, and stop. We kept on talking, because we'd ignore Homer most of the time, until he'd get out of hand. I called to him, "you're a noisy thing, trying to eavesdrop on us." I said, "I know you're out there." Creak, creak, creak, going up the stairs, wham, open the door, and wham up through the closet, since we had a closet with a cutout where you could go in the upper loft. That was his favorite route. Homer was gone because he was angry, we'd caught him eavesdropping on us.

He would pull those pranks and I would call his hand. He would always slam around after I had hollered at him because he was just like a child you would catch at something, or a child. He would just show his opinion; what he thought of me hollering at him.

I would sometimes go to the head of the stairs and say, "Stop clicking that light down there! I don't know how to take care of you, but I'm going to figure out a way." Then he would go click, click, click, click, just out of spite.

So I was conversant with him, and we just told him what we thought of him at the time, because we knew who was doing it and it wasn't our kids. So we accepted Homer. He was our friend, and we wonder what happened to him.

As far as our kids were concerned, they were aware. They could tell, because they were part of the household, and had to learn to live in a spooky house because of some of the things that were happening. Because we talked to him and because of things that were happening, naturally at first, they became a little ornery. There were only two times that the kids became a little concerned. My daughter was ironing upstairs, and she thought we had come in downstairs, and when it wasn't us, she thought it was someone else, and the craziness was going on downstairs, and because she couldn't tell whether it was Homer, or somebody else, she got scared. She took the two other children, who were younger, and she told them to get to their room, and she stood out there with a butcher knife, because she didn't know who was going to come up the stairs. When we came in, there hadn't been anybody and there wasn't anything disrupted. He didn't tear up the place, it just sounded like he was tearing up the place. When we came in, naturally everything was quiet and there was my daughter upstairs guarding the other children. So we looked, and of course, there wasn't anything. She said, "Well, you wouldn't believe what's been going on here." I said, "Yeah, we know." She said, "It scared me to death, because I didn't know what was happening." But again, he played a trick and got her scared, not hurting them, but got a reaction.

That's what he was always trying, to get a reaction. So they knew and when they'd be sitting around and the basement door would open, and creaking on the stairs, and hear that closet door upstairs, they'd just look up. They'd be doing their lessons or something, and they'd go on.

We knew what he was doing and we'd call his hand at it, but when the kids weren't there, sometimes he'd do other things. He would go take the potato chips or the cookies. Things disappeared. "All right, here's a box of Oreos that's gone. Now, what did you kids do with those Oreos? Did you eat them all?" "No, we didn't do it." Now the kids didn't go out, and they didn't have the money to buy and replace these Oreos. The next day the Oreos would be there. We had got on the kids and he'd bring them back. The potato chips, they'd say, "Where's the potato chips?" We'd say, "Well, you ate them all." "Daddy, we didn't open those potato chips." Well, I'd say, "The potato chips are gone. It had to be you all." They'd say, "It wasn't us." I'd say, "Well, it's Homer, then." Sure enough, they'd come back in and say, "Did you buy some more potato chips?" I'd say, "No, we're not buying any more potato chips." They'd say, "Well, what are these doing here?" We'd say, "Well, you know. Homer brought them back." We hadn't bought them and the kids weren't going out and buying any big bag of potato chips and putting them back on the shelf, and those sort of things happened all the time.

When they told the other kids, they'd say, "Well, how can you be in that house? It's got ghosts in it. Aren't you scared?" They weren't scared because they lived with Homer. They knew that Homer was there.

They're quite healthy about the whole thing, ₂nd because it was a pranky type of thing that would get them in trouble or make us ask them if it was them - a lot times they weren't around and he

52

was getting them in trouble.

There were just different things like that that he would start up with and then he'd quit, but no one would ever believe us. Homer went on this, and it's an odd thing, because Dennis Deitz asked me, "How long was he there?" Well, it never occurred to us until we put some dates down. When we were over at Farmer's Day in June 1970 was the beginning, and I remember the exact date he left in January 1978, because we had relatives coming in from Venezuela.

We were waiting for them at the house. We didn't know whether they would rent a car and come or someone was going to drop them off, or what. We were in the television room, as usual, nobody at home, and we heard this car pull up. We thought, "Well, there they are."

Well, it was a Volkswagen. A Volkswagen has a distinctive sound, and we wondered why in the world they had a Volkswagen. We didn't have any relatives who had a Volkswagen, so who was dropping Delores and Armando off?

So, we're sitting there, and of course, we knew they'd knock or come in. We heard the door open, and bam, bam, bam, up the stairs. We thought, "Well, maybe somebody's brought one of the teenagers home." Bam, crash, bam, back down the stairs, slam the door. in the Volkswagen, and off they go.

Well, I thought, Well, what in the world's happened, because we're expecting somebody." I went outside and of course, looked up and down the street and couldn't see any tail lights or anything. Homer caused all this racket and that car was gone. I never saw any lights.

The upshoot of it was that, after that point, we never heard any more from Homer. So I tell people that we question somewhat how Homer got here, that he left in a Volkswagen. We called him Jr., like we said, and in going back to that time period, in checking the dates, it was seven years, seven months, and seven days.

Now you can put any significance on that you want to, but we always told people when we were talking about Homer who understand. We didn't argue with them, we didn't try to defend, but we had fun telling people about Homer. They could believe it if they wanted to; but some of the things that he did, like the departure and his arrival, those time frames, the seven, seven, seven or his daddy over in Union with Dr. Maggie for a period of time that we couldn't put our finger on, and Dr. Maggie is deceased.

Where Homer went - we know where he came from, but I always tell people, "I don't know where he went, but he left in a Volkswagen." We wonder sometimes why he didn't come back, why he left, where he went. Remember, he was our friend, because I talked to him about some of the crazy things he'd do. I would tell him what I thought of him for doing some of them.

You know, it was seven and a half years of it. Well, seven, seven, seven.

Opal Haynes Anderson

JERRY'S VISION & OTHER STRANGE EVENTS

by Opal Haynes Anderson

Nearly everyone likes to hear ghost stories, especially the stories reputed to be true. We tended, as children, to believe most of the stories we heard. We believed ghosts lurked under beds, in closets and dark corners. With the wind whistling around the house, shaking windows and making eerie sounds, the only light being from the fireplace logs and perhaps moon light shining pale and eerie through a window made an ideal setting for spooks and goblin tales.

Growing up in the Hickory Flat area of Greenbrier County during the 1930's and 40's was a more relaxed way of life than today. There was no television and some radios still operated on battery power, used mostly for grown-ups to listen to the news. Milk, butter and eggs were still kept in ice boxes or in a spring house where cool, clear water ran through and kept them fresh as a modern refrigerator. Ice cream was enjoyed only on the Fourth of July and our food usually consisted of what we grew on the farm.

Our family as well as neighbors were up early and worked until dark or later, doing the endless farm chores. I don't recall many days when we weren't working. When our work day was over we manufactured our own amusement. Pie socials, cake walks, and square dancing were favorite Saturday night affairs, weather permitting. Other times we met at each others houses after church to play guitar, sing, or best of all, tell stories.

Almost everyone knew a ghost story that had been handed down and repeated for years. Lots of them claimed to have experienced first hand supernatural events. Perhaps they did. Parapsychologists say ghosts take different forms and this we believed. Some of the stories we heard say they saw forms, others heard sounds, others smelled strange odors, while others felt cold areas in otherwise warm places.

In the Autumn of 1886 several children in Russellville died from diphtheria including four from the Jerry Nutter household and four from the Robert Caperton and Mary Elinor "Nellie" Haynes family. The Haynes children were brothers and sister of my late father, Clarence L. Haynes. All four died in a 15 day period. Robert Jackson Haynes, who was seven (B. 7-11-79) died on November 6th. His ten year old sister, (4-9-76) Evert Genevra Haynes was the next to go five days later on November 11th. The family had barely gotten home from the funeral when six year old (9-22-80) George Roscoe died. The last to go was 11 year old Jermiah "Jerry" who died November 21st.

Jerry had not been told of the death of his best friend, Jerry Nutter, so it came as a surprise and shock when he inquired of his dad, "Why didn't you tell me Jerry Nutter had died?" When asked why he thought the Nutter boy was dead he replied, "I saw him with Genevra, Roscoe and Jackson, and I know they are dead."

The story Jerry told could hardly have been made up by an eleven year old. He said he was awakened by singing and the Nutter children, his sister and brothers came in the window and hovered around his bed before sitting on the bed. They said they were in a happy place and asked him to join them. They were not apparitions but distinct forms. He described the dress his sister wore and said she had the most beautiful comb in her hair. His six year old brother who talked only in a lisp before his death could talk plain as anyone After singing "the sweetest song" and talking with him, they floated out the window and disappeared over the tall woodland trees. They beckoned with their arms for him to follow until they were out of sight.

The doctor thought Jerry was getting better but Jerry insisted he didn't want to live and asked not to have further medication. He died a short time later.

Whether you believe in spirits or ghosts you are

bound to enjoy hearing eerie tales once in a while. Lots of folks believe in signs or tokens of impending disaster. Our community was no different. If a rooster crowed at night it meant disaster. A crow coming into a house signed impending doom for a member of the household. Once a few days before a neighbor died, a crow came into his house and could not be driven out.

One night mother saw a formation in the clouds over a neighbor's farm that looked like a small open casket. The next day we received news that the neighbor's baby had died that night.

Dad told of a time he was coming home late at night and saw something white in the road. As he got closer it raised up higher and higher. When he backed off to pick up a rock or stick to protect himself the white object lay back down. Of course, he knew you can't hit a ghost but he threw the rock anyway. Nothing happened, except that each time he approached the white form, it raised up higher and higher only to lie back down as he retreated. After several minutes of this, he decided to take a stick and walk right up to it. To his surprise he found yards and yards of white material lying in the road. In those days goods for stores farther up the ridge were carried in wagons and it seems a bolt of cotton material had fallen off the wagon as it went up a hill, unrolling as it fell. My parents kept the material for several years but never did find out who had lost it.

One of the Boley boys was returning home at night and as he approached the Cemetery Hill Church, he saw lights in the church and decided there were services going on. After parking his car he could still see lights in the building. Going to the church door he discovered the building dark and no one there.

Since there was no high school in the Russellville area until the late 1920's students had to attend school in other areas. Some stayed with relatives and attended Montgomery or East Bank High, others rode the train to Rainelle each day. A neighbor rented a house in Summersville so her children could attend Nicholas County High School. Others from the community boarded with her and attended school. It was a nice arrangement except the house she rented was haunted, or so they said.

Aunt Phenia told me about some of the strange happenings that went on in that house. "At first we thought some of the young folks were pulling pranks on us," she related to me, "but then strange things happened when none of them was around." She said the organ would play softly, like at a funeral, when no one was near it. Other times it sounded like every book had fallen from the book cases but on checking, none of the books was moved. Doors would open and shut by themselves and other strange sounds were heard. Needless to say they moved.

Another story made the rounds that a certain house was haunted. A man that studied law, as they used to say, lived and died there leaving all his books and papers spread about as he last used them. For years no one lived there and his things remained as he left them in an upstairs room. If his things were moved or bothered, the next day everything would be returned like he left them. Even the books would be opened to the same pages as before. Experts believe some ghosts don't know they are dead so their spirits remain on earth harmlessly.

I've always thought I'd like to get a good look and perhaps talk to a ghost. The nearest I ever came was when my grandmother was ill and later died. An aunt and uncle and I were staying with her. One morning I was making beds when I heard someone in the adjorning parlor. Thinking it was a sister, I spoke, but no one answered. The mistlike shape I saw came through a front unopened window, pranced a bit on the fireplace hearth, then exited through a closed outside door. Somehow I wasn't scared but my aunt said I was pale as a sheet when I came into the kitchen to ask if anyone had been in the parlor.

The indistinct form I described was thought to be that of an aunt, Ethel, who died before I was born. Why she may have come at that time we don't know. A couple of weeks later though, Grandmother died in the parlor, lay in state in front of the fireplace, and was taken out the same door I saw the form exit.

This same aunt was one of the first ladies to vote in the 1920 election. A short while before the election, she wasn't feeling well and another aunt and family were visiting her at the farm in Nicholas County. In 1920, there were no diners on trains so aunt Ethel was preparing a basket lunch for their trip on the early train from Nallen. While in the kitchen frying chicken, she heard a bump from the dark hallway that sounded "like a large sack of wool falling." A voice called out Ethel, Ethel, Ethel. Thinking one of the children had fallen down the stairs she hurried into the hall asking, "What do you want?"

Seeing no one on the dark hall she entered the parlor to find her sister crying. "Ethel, why did you answer that thing" her sister asked.

In her hurry to catch the train Ethel thought no more about the incident until later, but she never got a chance to question her sister further as to why she didn't think she should have answered the "thing". She died a few weeks later and Ethel never saw her again.

I've often wondered if aunt Nettie had seen and heard strange things before and if answering the "thing" may have had something to do with her untimely death. Did she have powers we were unaware of? Did she really appear to me to warn of grandmother's pending death. For sure I'll never know the answer.

A favorite teller of stories was an uncle that lived on Cabin Creek. One story he related was that of a girl who'd given birth to a baby and left it in a worked out coal mine to die. Most any night, one could hear the baby crying. Another story he told was that a face could be seen peering from a window in an old boarded up, abandoned mill, and a train could be seen and heard running through a section where there were no railroad tracks.

Another story making the rounds was that a certain neighbor living in the area around the turn of the century was a witch. The woman was supposed to be in contact with evil spirits and possessed supernatural powers. No one dared cross her for fear of having a hex put on them. She was supposed to have obtained these bewitching powers by selling her soul to the devil. She placed one hand on the soles of her feet, the other hand on the top of her head and declared "I sell my soul to the devil." We were also told anyone could do this but we weren't brave enough to try. Strange things always seemed to be happening that were attributed to the witch. She made the cows give bloody milk, broke animals legs, set houses and barns afire causing confusion in general.

One occasion, a Mr. Brown was deer hunting when a doe walked out of the brush right in front of him. No way could he have missed hitting the animal, but he did so at point blank range. While reloading his mountain rifle, the deer just stood and watched. After missing a second time he became suspicious, as the deer still flirted around near him.

Believing the deer to actually be the witch in disguise he sat on a log pondering what he should do. Everyone knows you can't shoot a witch with a lead bullet and not sure of her intentions as the doe played around him switching her tail, he noticed a bunch of splinters where the log had broken. Keeping one eye on the witch-doe he again loaded his rifle with gun powder but instead of adding a bullet, he tamped a handful of the wood slivers into the gun barrel. This time when he shot the splinters hit home and the deer took off at a gallop bellowing something awful.

The next day he stopped by the witches house on some excuse but was told she could not come to the door as she was laid up from injuries received when she fell over a fence and got splinters in her backside.

After my grandfather died in 1901 there was some dispute among the heirs as to how his property should be divided. He had left a will but some were not happy with what had been left to them. On advice of some busybody, one of my aunts went to see a sorceress to try to contact her late father via a familiar spirit. The sorceress had a large metal horn that one could talk through and reach the spirit of the departed.

After gathering in a dark room one could ask questions. It is said the horn became so heavy one could not hold it when the spirits began to speak.

Whether she really contacted a spirit or not I'll never know but some male voice did answer her question by saying, "I no longer am of the world and will make no decisions as to what should be done on earth." The aunt nearly had a nervous breakdown after the experience.

One of the favorite stories handed down and repeated time after time for years was about the local farmer who had served in the Civil War before settling near Meadow River in our area. If I ever knew, I don't remember what he had done that made him the meanest person in these parts. But he was even more evil than the man who killed pack peddlers and burned their bodies on brush piles.

The farmer became ill and was not expected to live. Neighbor men took turns sitting up with him at nights so his family could get some rest from nursing him. One night a Mr. Moore and Mr. Jones were doing the honors when late in the night they heard a noise outside that sounded like rattling and dragging chains. They saw an object walk by an open window and Mr. Jones ran out a door. The other man, being behind the bed had nowhere to run so he sat on the floor and watched. He said the most horrible creature he ever saw, with a face that surpassed all ugly evil, came and wrestled with the struggling man in the bed. After the devilish creature left, they found their patient to be dead as a mackerel."

On checking they saw the floor was singed in the shape of footprints where the creature had walked in and where he stood by the bed the burn marks went deep into the boards. People went for years to see the devil's footprints in the singed floor boards. Neither of the men doubted that their visitor was satan and that he came to take the evil farmer away.

Storytelling seems to be a lost art in society today, but in other times we shared good times, good stories, good friends and neighbors.

You may not have heard many ghost stories but we've all had strange feelings you can't explain and there are not always rational explanations for everything that happens. Spirits and ghosts could be the answer.

James Godfrey

JAMES GODFREY STORY

My wife and I were visiting in an old house near Fincastle, Va. We were sleeping in one of the four bedrooms upstairs. All of the doors to the bedrooms were closed. The lady of the house (the only other person in the house) was unable to climb the stairs. In the middle of the night, it was quite dark as the house was in the country, no street lights to cast shadows. I awoke and saw a shimmering golden light in the far corner of the room. It faded, and I felt the cover of my blanket being lifted and then dropped, and the light disappeared. The next morning, all of the doors to the bedrooms upstairs were standing wide open.

Another time, in the same house, four of us were playing cards in the living room. I was seated so that I looked directly into the hallway, which was dark. I saw a yellowish mass float by the door in the hallway. I asked if the lady of the house had ever seen "Uncle Ed," the ghost who was known to be in the house. She said she had never seen it, only heard noises that it made nearly every night, as if looking for something. Not being one who believes in ghosts, I have been unable to determine just what I saw, other than it was a ghost. I hope that you might want to use these two instances some time. They certainly were real, not imaginative, and unexplainable.

APRIL DAWN
PERSINGER'S STORY
Age: 11

April is a young friend of mine I met when I spoke to her fourth grade class. She is now 12 years old, she hopes to be a writer and we keep in touch.

Thank you April for your contribution to my book.

The Author

The other day, my best friend and I went to our church's Young Peoples meeting. We went way down to the Manse to play volleyball. Mandy and I didn't want to play, so we walked back to the upper building where we always have the meetings. Now, it was a pretty long way from where they were so we took the keys to get in. When we got there, we started talking about the rock-a-thon the Young Peoples had a few nights before. They had told stories, one of which was true: in the same exact building we were in, there was a girl who got trapped in a fire and died.

We started getting kind of scared but after awhile, we just forgot all about it and went outside. Then, all of a sudden, I couldn't find the keys. We got very confused and thought we'd left them in the building. Again I felt in my back pocket and they were there. Now, I never told Mandy that they were not in my back pocket before but when I felt the next time they were there. I just acted like I had them all the time.

Then we started hearing, or at least I thought we heard, footsteps going through the building. However, no one besides us had been in there. Then we heard someone talking in there, but we never found out what it was. We haven't told anyone either.

Also, Mrs. Coots told us today in class something that no one ever believed.

She said that on this one road, there had been some teenagers driving and they tried to pass a car and were killed in a crash. She and Mrs. Nolan were driving on that very road one night. This crash had happened many years before and people had said that you could see that car and it would disappear. She was driving and all at once a car passing another one came on her side and it was in the way, so she got mad and slowed down. Then she looked and it was gone, so she asked Mrs. Nolan if, she had seen a car just then. She said she had, and thought maybe it had turned off and they hadn't seen it. They went up to where it passed the other car and there were cliffs, one on each side, so they couldn't have turned off!

I just thought I'd tell you those stories. They really are true, for I wouldn't make anything like that up. I thought you may like them, however.

APRIL DAWN PERSINGER

THE ASHTON GHOST
by Joyce Moore and Martha Cross Sargent

Grandmother was born Mary May Hersman in Pliny, WV, daughter of James Madison and Sarah Lieulla Curry Hersman. James Hersman left his family when our Grandmother was a small child, leaving her mother to support them as best she could, working as a midwife and herb doctor. The children were raised in a deeply religious home, and Grandmother devotedly adhered to these principles all her life.

She had to leave the farm as a young woman, and earn her own way. She took a job as a domestic helper with a family in Ashton, WV. There she took care of two children and helped with all the work, for room and board and a small wage, part of which she sent to her mother each month.

She later married Washington Milton Willis and lived the remainder of her married life on Laurel Creek Road, at Waverly, WV.

Grandmother would climb into bed with us to tell a ghost story, though she was tired from her long day of work on the farm. Drawing on a wealth of information stored in her mind of times, places and people long past, she told wonderful stories. One that always elicited a squeal of fear from each of us was a ghost story from her own experience. We did not doubt the truth of her story as children, nor would we ever.

"When I was a girl," she would begin...

Grandmother was restless that night, just two weeks after starting to work in the house at Ashton. The place was still strange to her as it would be to a young girl away from home for the first time in her life. She had bathed, pulled her long blond hair into a braid at the back of her head (her religion forbade the cutting of a woman's hair), and had said her prayers before lying down in her room. She was unable to sleep and had lain awake for several hours. The others in the house-hold had gone to bed long before.

She heard a muffled sound in the kitchen beneath her room, as if a chair was being pulled and scraped across the wooden floor. She listened closely and heard a soft tapping which went on for some time.

She rose quietly from her bed and crept down the stairs, careful not to wake the others. She wondered if perhaps one of the children was out of bed, hungry or ill. The little boy she cared for was a "sickly" child. As she neared the kitchen doorway, the tapping sound grew louder.

A woman was seated at the kitchen table. A canopy of diffused light moved over and about her, like a candle flame flickering, and the ordinary furnishings of the kitchen became unsubstantial and seemed to disappear into the gloomy recesses of the room.

The woman was young, not much older than Grandmother, and was dressed in old-fashioned clothing. She wore a mourning dress of stiff black fabric, the neckline high and tight, the skirt floor-length, and high-topped shoes with many buttons. Her dark hair was caught up in a black ribbon at the nape of her neck. She wore no jewelry or ornament of any kind. She sat very erect on the chair, her head bent intently to her work, hands moving rapidly over the keyboard of a typewriter on the table before her.

The woman's face was poignant, a tear sliding silently down her cheek now and then.

Grandmother watched for a while, half-hidden by the doorway, before summoning all her courage to ask, "Who are you?"

There was no response from the figure at the table.

Grandmother asked again, "Who are you and why are you here?"

The woman did not answer.

Grandmother stood transfixed as the pitiful figure worked on in the eerie light, through the dark hours, until the first rays of dawn appeared, then faded away into nothingness, her illumination and her typewriter fading away with her.

The kitchen resumed it's normal appearance with the daylight, and Grandmother decided not to tell anyone what she had seen, fearing they might think her daft or possessed by the devil.

The ghost appeared to her several times as the weeks and months went by. She prayed each night that she would solve the mystery of the spectral figure at the table. An answer to her prayers was provided through her daily Bible reading.

Grandmother knew what she should ask the next time the woman appeared. She waited impatiently, for several nights, until, once more, the scraping sound came from the kitchen below her room.

Grandmother ran quietly down the stairs and into the kitchen, where the woman played out the scene, the soft wavering light surrounding her, the fingers tapping incessantly. She stepped farther into the room and walked close to the table. She spoke softly to the woman, "In the Name of The Father, The Son, and The Holy Ghost, who are you and why are you here?"

The woman stopped typing, and turned slowly in her chair to look at Grandmother with tear-filled eyes.

"My name is Marietta. I fear that my father has been murdered and I cannot rest until I know who killed him and where they buried his body; nor can I mourn him properly. I have to do this work until I find the answers in this world."

She gazed at Grandmother a moment longer, as if seeking an answer from her, then resumed her work tapping and tapping, fingers moving over the keyboard.

Grandmother continued to see the woman as long as she was employed by the people at Ashton. She could never understand the significance of the typewriter, an unusual appliance to see in that day and age, or what the woman could possibly have done to deserve such a penance. It puzzled Grandmother that the ghost did not appear to anyone else in the house. She never attempted to speak to the woman again, for she felt somehow that the answers would always be the same.

Grandmother eventually left the family at Ashton and moved on to another. She would wonder for the rest of her life if that poor soul was ever given an answer or respite from her sad vigil, or if she was still there, typing on through the nights into infinity.

Our Grandmother has long since passed away, but she still reminds us that there are other places, somewhere, that we cannot understand. She appears from time to time, sitting in her rocking chair. Her head is bent forward, bird-like, bright blue eyes peering down the hall, as if waiting for someone to appear.

We do not feel that Grandmother is bound to this earth because of some unresolved circumstances in her life, like the woman in her story, but rather a need to be near her beloved family.

Grandmother used to say, "Child, did you ever hear of a ghost harming anyone in any way? Of course you haven't. I think we are afraid of them just because we cannot explain them. Perhaps they're only angels."

GRANDMA'S STORY
by Kevin P. Anderson

This story was told to me by my grandmother. I believe the time period to be sometime in the 1930's at Gatewood, near Oak Hill, W. Va. She said that one evening she noticed two men who appeared to be digging a grave on the hillside near her home. A lantern could be seen burning and sounds of digging could be heard as they worked through the night. They did not work during the day, but as soon as dusk came around, the men could be seen again. This apparently went on for about a week when my grandmother, her curiosity finally getting the best of her, decided to walk over to the spot where all the digging was taking place. When she arrived at the place, not a hole could be found, not even a place where ground had been disturbed. the evenings passed peacefully ever since and the "grave diggers" were never seen again. My grandmother had no reason for what she had seen, only that she was sure of what she saw, a ghost.

Now, below this same ridge is a very old house which still stands. This house apparently has been visited by a ghost or two. It has been said that one family has seen a ghost of an old woman roaming the house. Once the father, who had fallen asleep on the couch, was awakened to see this ghost walking past him from one room to the next. After this sighting, the ghost was seen doing the same for a time, until something supposedly happened that even I find somewhat difficult to believe. Some of the children were playing upstairs when they heard the youngest girl yell for help. What they saw was the little girl being pulled by the hand into the closet by the ghost of the old woman. The elder sister, about 12 or 13 years old, took the little girl by the other hand trying to pull her back into the room, when she finally yelled out, "LET HER GO!" The ghost turned loose of her and disappeared

They later asked the little girl about it and she only said that the ghost's hand was very cold. I'm not sure, but I don't think that the ghost has been seen since.

While I'm on the same mountain I have one more story I find worth telling. Remember in the 70's when all the UFO sightings seemed to be going around? Well it seems that a UFO was seen that appeared to crash into the side of the mountain. The UFO had been seen by several people and one man claimed to see a man in a spacesuit leaning with his head and arm against a tree. Quickly returning home, the State Police was called to investigate. The only thing they found was a hole in the tree line where some branches were broken out, supposedly from the crashing UFO. Shortly after it happened, I did see the place where the limbs were torn out, which could be seen from quite a distance.

My uncle Moxie told me a story of a man who threw a rock and killed a boy. Throughout the next month the man would complain of rocks coming out of nowhere, as if someone was throwing them at him. Within a month he too was hit in the head with a rock and killed. The murderer was never found.

Once my good friend Dean Workman, his two uncles, Larry and Mike, and his two cousins, Randy and Scott, went coon hunting on Cotton Hill in Fayette County. It was the day before Christmas Eve about 9:00 p.m. Dean, Larry and Randy took a jeep and Mike and Scott took their truck. The old logging road was very muddy on the way up and near the top they noticed an old junk car just off the side of the road. They passed the junk car about 100 yards and parked their own vehicles. They walked over a ridge and started down an old logging road for about a mile when they stopped to rest. Larry decided to continue in the direction they were headed while the rest waited. A long time passed and Larry did not return so Dean figured Larry must have gone the wrong way. Dean and the rest went the other way for about a mile when they came to the vehicles. Dean decided to take the jeep and look for Larry when he discovered he did not have the keys for the jeep, only for the truck. After going through the keys he did have, he found one that would fit the jeep. After working with it, he got it to work the ignition, only to find the battery dead. Unknown to him, Randy went up the road to the old junk car to look for some jumper cables. All of a sudden Dean heard what sounded like a howl and then a scream. Dean looked up to see Randy come running back from the junk car, slipping and sliding in the mud and screaming "Dean! Dean!" while the mining light dragged behind him. Randy ran to the jeep, got inside and closed the door, his face white as a ghost. Dean, thinking that something had happened to Larry, tried to calm Randy and find out what was wrong. Randy said, "Dean, the car is full of dead bodies!". A chill came over Dean and he decided he would wait for Larry to return and they would all go up to the car to investigate. When they went up to the car, it did have bodies in it, one with its face pressed against the glass with a fifth of liquor on the seat. These bodies weren't dead, only drunk and passed out, I guess getting tanked up for the upcoming Christmas holiday.

Bob Jacobus

Bob Jacobus holds a B.S. from Purdue University in Wildlife Science and a Master of Theology from Liberty Bible College. He has been a successful farmer, coal miner, and teacher. Bob is currently operator of West Virginia Department of Natural Resource's Mobile Wildlife Exhibit.

GHOSTS AT BRIGADOON

by Bob Jacobus

Under the morning shadows of Kate's Mountain in Greenbrier County rests the beautiful farm Brigadoon. I had the good fortune of being its caretaker for a season.

Now the play "Brigadoon" had a central theme, "only believe". Such is the case with ghosts, in order to embrace them...only believe.

I had just finished a Master of Theology before coming to Brigadoon. How can a trained theologian only believe? Simple...put the situation in theological terms. There are good ghosts and there are bad ghosts. There are good spirits and there are bad spirits. There are angels and there are demons. These are all labels for the same thing.

The first week at Brigadoon the presence of ghosts were quite clear. Now there were both kinds present so it was a bit confusing at first. Good ghosts are ministering spirits from a theological point of view. They make you welcome and at peace. The other kind makes one feel the coldness of fear.

This situation was definitely out of my comfort zone, but I had lived under similar conditions before. The Bible says that a devil cannot touch one who accepts the blood of Christ as protection, I was covered! What I didn't know was that I was the physical interface of a spiritual battle that had been waged at the farm for years.

The caretaker before me lost an eye in a "freak accident". I almost lost an eye on day three. No coincidence.

It felt so good to be at Brigadoon, but then it was so frightening at times. Only trusting in the blood of Jesus brought peace to the heart.

The big battle happened on night five. Brigadoon was peaceful that day and going to bed was no problem. Sleep came easily.

I awoke suddenly in the middle of darkness ..there was a strange noise under my bed...it sounded as if something or somebody was crawling on their belly. It happened!!!

The bed flew apart as if some giant had laid on his back, put his feet in the middle of the bed, and kicked straight up with all his might. The only trouble was I was still in it!

As I collected myself off the floor anger began to steam from my spirit. An unknown tongue came from my mouth and began to pray, "Lord, I plead the blood of Jesus on my life and on this home. I command in the name of Jesus that all spirits in rebellion to the Lord must flee Brigadoon. Lord set your ministering spirits here at every corner post so that your peace may rest here. Protect me and guard me from your enemies which are also mine, Amen."

Two days later this whole experience was considered just a bad dream. It had reality about it, but what sane person would "only believe"? Then a letter came from New Orleans, 1000 miles away. "Bob, I feel that you should start believing in God for protection. You probably are already, but strengthen your faith in His word for protection about you. Like the protection in the Blood of Jesus, and the angels, and the Word of God. Meditate in Psalm 91. Bob, I really don't understand why I am telling you this, but I think and believe you should do as I've said. I have prayed a couple of times in the past few days that Jesus would protect you."

Brigadoon became quite a place of peace, I will always cherish my days there. The bad ghosts came back after I left, they always do. Remember that their desire for a home is not a wooden building, but they want to haunt the house of one's soul...Only believe.

Margaret Elswick

THE GHOSTLY COUCH
by Margaret Elswick

My father-in-law "pappaw" took up with a woman young enough to be his daughter. His wife had died several months back. Since he had waited on her hand and foot, everyone was glad for him.

This woman had a bad temper and carried a gun. We just knew something bad was going to happen.

One evening a fight started between them after a quarrel over an old truck. She threatened to shoot him. He ran inside and sat down on the couch. About that time, she came in the room and shot him seventeen times.

While cleaning out the house, we decided to clean the stains off the couch and take it home. We placed the couch in the room and put a throw over the stain that wouldn't come out. Then strange things began to happen.

One night we saw pappaw sitting on his porch with a white shirt on, smoking a pipe. We watched until he disappeared. A few nights later we saw the figure again in the same position.

We then began to notice that a cushion on the couch would be moved around. Once the throw was in the floor.

One day a lady was visiting us. We began talking about the strange things that had been happening. She was sitting on the couch at the time and suddenly let out a scream and ran out the door. Everyone else in the room started to run out of the room. When we all calmed down she began to tell what had frightened her so badly.

She said the feel of a cold hand around her neck was causing her to be unable to breathe. We went inside, carried the couch out and burned the thing. We never saw or heard anything after that but it was a long time before anyone would want to set in the parlor by themselves.

THE OLD LADY WHO LOVED CATS

by Margaret Elswick

There was an old lady who lived about two miles from my uncle. Neighbors were not close but we would visit her whenever we made our trips back to see Uncle Joe. She loved cats and took in every stray that came by. Each cat had a name and its own dish.

This lady didn't have much to live on but always made sure that her cats were fed. Everyone wondered what would happen to the cats if she should die.

One day Uncle Joe went up the holler to see if everything was OK and if she needed anything. When he found the cats running around outside the door, he knew something was wrong.

He found her very sick. She said please feed the cats because she was so worried about them. After feeding them, he went back inside. She was very still. Going over to the bed he realized she was dead.

The funeral was held at home, everyone wondered what would happen to the cats. Some said they would take care of themselves. No one went back to the house for several weeks.

One day, Uncle Joe went up the hollow and met an old white crippled cat. He couldn't remember ever seeing it before. When he got up to her house, there were no cats around only the old white cat which followed him around as if trying to tell him something.

He went back down the hollow not thinking too much about the cat until several neighbors began to talk about the cat appearing out of nowhere. Sometimes when the women of the town would be out picking greens the cat would trail behind them. No one gave a thought that it might be a ghost until one night a scratching was heard at the back door. It made Uncle Joe think of the times back that a knock would be heard and the old lady would be there.

As he opened the door, there stood the old white crippled cat looking so sad. He put some milk out on the porch for the stray cat, knowing that is what the old lady would have done. When he got back to the door nothing was there. Then several neighbors began to feel uneasy every time they saw the cat. People began to wonder if it could be the old lady in the form of a cat.

The annual picnic was held at the church and everyone was discussing the strange actions of the old crippled cat. It looked so bad that the children were beginning to be afraid.

Out of nowhere there appeared the cat at the church yard where the food had been put on tablecloths lying on the ground. The only thing that puzzled them about whether the cat really was a ghost of their neighbor was the crippled leg. Then a lady who had visited with the old lady just before her death started talking. She said the lady had fallen over one of the cats that day and injured her ankle. By then everyone was blaming themselves for not taking one or two of the cats.

This old cat was listening to them or so they thought. They began to whisper and one man started to go toward her. When he got near her she ran to the grave of the old lady and disappeared, never to be seen again.

That taught a lesson to the neighbors. Always feed and be kind to any stray animal because who knows-it may be a spirit of someone who is not quite ready to pass over.

Martha Cross Sargent
1990

THE MYSTERY WEEPING WILLOW TREE

by Margaret Elswick

In a small mining town stood a house that had been quite empty for several months. Several families had moved in but didn't stay for long. All kinds of sounds were heard; chairs turning over, dishes breaking and the sounds of a baby crying.

Grandpa said, "We need a bigger house and I don't believe all those tales." So he moved the furniture in and the family got ready for bed that night. The first night nothing happened. Of course, that made Grandpa believe the "tall tales" was someone's imagination.

Next morning, as the family ate breakfast, everyone began to talk about being pleased with their bedrooms. In those days, there was no front room which is now used for our living rooms. Most rooms had two double beds and if the family was large some would sleep on the floor.

This house had enough bedrooms for everyone. One of the kids said, "I'm not afraid of ghosts." That night, bed covers began sliding off the bed. Dishes were breaking in the kitchen, and the sound of a baby crying was coming from the attic.

After inquiring around as to the previous occupants of the house before the noise began, it was learned that a family lived there for several years but no one knew much about them except that the woman liked to work in the garden and the baby would be in a basket beside her. When the husband came home from work, everyone would go inside. Sometimes you would hear him cursing and throwing things. The baby would cry and the woman would beg him to stop. Supposedly he had a bad temper and would stop off at a bootlegging joint and drink before coming home.

The mother and baby weren't seen out for several days and the father had reported for work but no one thought anything about it because that wasn't unusual since they always kept to themselves.

Finally the mine boss went to check on the man because he hadn't been to work. Finding the door unlocked, he pushed it open and went inside. Everything was a mess; dishes broken and clothes thrown everywhere. No one knew what happened.

Everyone decided the man killed his family, did away with their bodies and left.

Grandpa began to search around the house and couldn't find anything. He then went up into the attic. There was a small box with a couple of toys and several aprons. He brought the box down to the back yard and after digging a hole and burying the box no more noises were heard in the house. No one ever found out what happened to the family.

Grandpa said the restless spirits were buried with the box. A weeping willow tree came up where the box was planted but it remained a mystery how the tree got there and why it was a weeping willow.

June Haydon

SISTERS A'RIDING

by June Haydon

Note: This event happened to my grandmother, Virginia DeBusk, who lived in Washington County, Virginia. She told the story to my mother and it was passed down to me. It occurred around 1890.

Virginia was alone on the farm that day, with the exception of her year old daughter and five year old son. It had rained for days so there was no possibility of taking the children outdoors. However, Virginia had more than enough to do, what with churning and daily washing and the children to mind. She was often lonely while her husband was away teaching school, but never idle.

On that particular day, she woke up feeling as if something was about to happen. Swiftly she decided that her sisters, Carrie and Maud, must be coming for a visit. Although they lived only twenty miles away, she had not seen them for a couple of months. Yes, it was more than time for a visit. So certain was she that she opened the windows in the guest room and made up the bed. Then she put one of her famous pound cakes in the oven and hurried around, 'slicking' up the house.

Some time later she put the baby down for her noon-time nap and went into the parlor to make sure all was in order. Glancing out the window, she saw her sisters. They were riding sidesaddle and headed for the barn.

"Roscoe," Virginia called to her son. "Run down and open the gate for your aunt Maud and aunt Carrie. That way they can ride their horses right up to the barn. Try to stay out of the mud."

Her sturdy little son ran to do as he was told. Just then Virginia smelled her cake and hurried back to the kitchen to rescue it. About that time the baby woke up and needed to be changed. Virginia soothed the child and eased her back into her cradle to finish her nap. Then she slipped out of the bedroom.

Roscoe appeared at her side.

"Where are your aunts?" she asked.

"They weren't there, Mama. I waited and waited by they didn't come."

"What on earth? I saw them ride by the house."

Bewildered, Virginia took Roscoe's hand and the two went downstairs. Just then they heard a horse's hooves thundering down the road. Virginia opened the front door and saw her brother dismounting.

"Fred?" she said, puzzled. "How good to see you. Come in..."

"No, this isn't a visit, Jennie," he said in a voice she had never heard before. "I bear terrible news. Carrie and Maud started out this morning to come to see you. When they reached the middle of the bridge, it collapsed and they were swept away. We recovered them...they both drowned."

POPPIE'S GHOST

by Rosalie Scott

The holler was spooky on dark nights when I walked the few yards from the mouth to the second house which was my home place. My dog "Tippie" came to meet me and kept the beasts of the night away. I sometimes didn't have a flashlight and couldn't see my hand before my face. It felt good to get inside the house although back then in the late thirties we never locked the doors.

After I moved to town and away from the home place, I decided to go back and stay a night after Mom and Dad died. My brother lived alone there and was glad to see me. I parked the car down the holler and walked up. The evening was cool with a misty rain of fall.

After a meal of squirrel gravy and biscuits cooked on the ole wood burnin' stove, we turned in early. We had a fire in the front room grate and I lay watching shadows quiver on the ceiling from the blazes that wormed their way through the ashes from the 'banked' fireplace. If cinders were scooped on the grate fire of coal, it kept all night for easy startin' in the morning.

After drifting off to sleep, I dreamed Pappa came to me, wanting to convey a message. I said, "Wait, I'm in a hurry." When I returned, he was gone. I dreamed in vivid color.

The following day, I took the customary hike to the head of the branch and renewed childhood memories. Later, I placed flowers on the graves of Mom and Pop. A wind came up all of a sudden and whistled mournfully on the plains nearby. I felt a chill in my bones.

Pappa'd always teased me about the whippoor-will and told me it said, "Get that girl." When we walked home from Sunday night church, he'd say, "See them green eyes shinin' from the thicket?" Papa was always finding things that I'd lost as a child.

91

I searched the house for keepsakes before time to light the old oil lamp and I could feel Pappa very near. This evening I knew he would come in spirit. Sure nuff, a thump resounded on the stairway. When I went to look, there was the last doll he had bought me with tousled hair and its green and pink dress ragged with age. It had fallen from a low precipice and didn't break. I picked it up gently and saw the blue eyes open. Just as I hugged the doll close, steps thumped up three stairs and I saw a shadow disappear. It couldn't have been my brother for he was on the porch gathering kinlin' for the fire. Pappa had been there and found the doll for me.

The next day, as I was gathering my belongings for the journey back to town, my brother said, "Where did you find that doll?" I replied, "Pappa found it for me."He said, "Likely story." When I said, "Bye, I'll be back again." He replied as I hugged him good-bye, "I have felt his presence and Mom's too, but she was always so quiet and shy. Their spirits are in this place but I'm not afraid to live alone." Seems he looked more like Pappa than ever before.

Margaret "Peggy" Miller

CONNIE AND THE OUIJA BOARD

by Margaret (Peggy) Miller

As I was growing up on a farm in rural New Hampshire I heard many stories of strange happenings. For generations my ancestors had passed on to their children tales of ghosts and unexplainable events, and I developed a love for these oft repeated yarns, causing me to have many chills and thrills.

Not all the stories were old, as some of these strange events happened in my life time.

The latest I heard about happened to my sister-in-law, Connie, who told me the following story when we visited them in Maryland.

While we were shopping, the children wanted to buy a Ouija Board. Connie said, "I hope they don't buy that! I had such a strange experience with one that they almost scare me."

When she was in high school she had gone to a church summer camp. One night after she had gone to sleep one of the girls woke her up to tell her the Ouija Board was saying, "I want Connie, I want Connie."

She got up and started using the Ouija Board. It told her, "Your uncle (giving the name) is a prisoner in a Soviet camp in Siberia." She was given a telephone number to call in Washington, D.C. Connie said she laughed and told the girls she didn't even have an uncle by that name.

When she got home she told her parents about what the Ouija Board had told her, and her mother ran from the room crying.

Her father told her, "Your mother did have a brother by that name. He was captured or lost in Germany during World War II. He and your mother were very close, and she was so distraught that she still refuses to even mention his name."

Her father told her not to call the number and never to mention this again, for it was just too traumatic for her mother.

One of the many jobs my father had was that of a logger in the mountains of northern Vermont. He moved my mother and four older siblings to a little house in Vermont that was near enough so that he could go home from the logging camp on weekends. This was in the 1930's before I was born. My mother said that it was very cold that winter and that they lived in an isolated area without a telephone. My father drove their old car to the logging camp, so this left my mother without transportation or means of communication except through a neighbor down the road who had a telephone.

One day the neighbor came to my parent's house and delivered the message that my uncle had been killed in an automobile accident in Concord, New Hampshire, and that they were to get back to Concord as soon as possible. Well, this was during the week that my mother had no way of communicating this to my father who was miles away at the logging camp. My mother said she was worried sick about how she was going to get the message to my father, and that she lay awake most of the night picturing my dead uncle.

Early the next morning there was a knock on her door. When she answered she found a man standing there who she had never seen. He told her that he had come for my father's lunch. My mother was surprised because my father ate all of his meals at the logging camp. She told the stranger this, but he replied that my father had sent him after his lunch. My mother told him that all she had were some cold biscuits left over from the night before. He said to put them in a bag. This she did. When she gave him the bag of biscuits she asked him if he would tell my father that his brother had been killed the day before, and that he had to come home so they could get back to New Hampshire for the funeral.

That night my father arrived home. They bundled up my brother and sisters and set out for Concord. While driving along my father turned to my mother and asked her who that man was that she sent to tell him about his brother's death. My mother told him that she had never seen the man before, and that he had said that he had been sent by my father to get his lunch. My father said, "I've never seen that man before in my life."

THE BLUE LIGHT

by Carol McClung

I am a nurse and the story I would like to share with you, happened to me shortly after I graduated nursing school and went to work at a nursing home.

I was working the midnight shift in a nursing home the first time I heard about "The Blue Light". This particular night I was in the medicine room with the door open when I heard this awful scream. I stepped out to see what was wrong. The scream had come from a cleaning lady, who was by this time crying uncontrollably and was white as a sheet; there were two nurses' aides there too which appeared to be upset. I asked what was wrong, the cleaning lady replied, "I just saw the Blue Light". I asked what was the Blue Light? They all exclaimed at once, you mean you don't know about the Blue Light? I said no, I don't guess I do. Well this is the story they told to me. According to them the Blue Light is a Phenomenon that is seen at the nursing home before someone dies, just a big blue flash of light, after which someone always dies. Both of the aides said they had seen it many times as they both worked there many years and death is a common visitor at a nursing home. Well, I did not necessarily believe this but they were pretty upset and me being new on the job, I just listened to their little story and kept my opinion to myself as I always thought there was a logical explanation for everything. Even though the next day a little old lady died, I still thought death comes often in a nursing home, just a coincidence.

Then about two months later at about 4 a.m., one of my patients became very ill and I was trying to get her transferred out to the hospital and things were very busy and hectic. I was rushing around making arrangements and as I was coming out of the patient's room suddenly there was this great big flash of light, it startled me so I stopped and said "What was that?". The aide with me, knowing I never really believed their story, just smiled sweetly at me and replied, "You just now saw the Blue Light"; needless to say that was the last thing I wanted to hear with a critically ill patient on my hands, but still I thought to myself a light bulb or something had blown, but I did not have time to ponder the situation just yet, as my patient came first.

After the patient had been safely transferred to the hospital and I had time to investigate-investigate I did-but to no avail every light was burning and I could find no reason for that big flash of blue light. And about my very sick patient, she did not die, she got well and is still living today. But a few days later we lost another kindly old lady down that same hallway where I had seen the Blue Light. Regarding the Blue Light I only know what I saw and I know what followed a few days later. I'm still not sure just what I think about the Blue Light and I will leave that up to your own imagination. But, as for those aides, there's not a doubt in their minds. The Blue Light means a death will follow.

Betty Burns Lusher

A BALL OF LIGHT

by Betty Burns Lusher

In 1903 there was an epidemic of smallpox in Huntington. People were dying like flies. Not many people were on the streets. Everyone stayed inside to keep from getting this contagious disease. But that didn't seem to stop it. There was an almost constant rattle of wagons on the streets. The "dead wagons" draped in black, stopped at houses that had a black cloth on the door, to pick up the dead. The wagons draped in white, stopped where there was a white cloth to take the sick and dying to the "Pest House." Here overworked doctors did the best they could with very little to work with. They had very few people to help them, only those few who had already had smallpox and recovered. The best they could do didn't seem to be enough. More died than got well.

Grandpaw Bias-William Alfred Bias-got sick with smallpox. Grandmaw Bias didn't want him to go to the "Pest House" but she had to think of the rest of the family. She hung a white rag on the front porch and soon a wagon stopped. They carried Grandpaw out and gently placed him in the wagon. He waved and threw a kiss. Grandmaw stood on the porch and cried as she watched the wagon move down the street and out of sight. She never saw him again. Two days later, an official came to inform her of his death and to find out the cemetery and lot number where she wanted him buried. There could be no funeral. He just told her that he would be buried sometime the next day when they got to him.

Some of Grandpaw's boys decided to be there. Early the next morning they walked from Fifth Ave. and 26th Street out to Spring Hill Cemetery. They were not allowed inside the gates so they stood up on the ridge beside the road and waited. From here they could see the family plot and they would know when he was buried. The hours passed. They watched men digging graves all over the cemetery. They watched the "dead wagon" bring loads of caskets to the gates and stack them there. Then other men would read the names and lot numbers on the caskets and take them to the proper spot and bury them. No funeral. Not even a prayer. They just put them in the ground, covered them and moved on to the next one.

The day dragged on and still they waited. Finally about dusk the men stopped at Grandpaw's grave site. As they dropped the casket into the ground, Grandpaw's sons bowed their heads and recited the 23rd Psalm and the Lord's Prayer. That was the only funeral he had. It was over quickly and the men moved on to the next grave. The boys stood for a few minutes and then started home. They hadn't gone but a few steps when one of the boys turned for one last look. He stopped and called to the others. "Look! Look at Paw's grave!" They all turned and there on Paw's grave was a ball of light. It looked like it had come out of the grave! While they watched, it rose and moved up the hill and came to a stop about 30 feet ahead of them. It was a glowing ball of light about the size of a man's head. It seemed to float about four or five feet off the ground. The boys looked at each other and then back at the ball of light. It was still there. They didn't know if they should run or stand still. If they did run, should they run at or away from it? At last, one of the boys took a step or two toward it. It moved away from him.

They started to follow it. It stayed just ahead of them and moved on out the ridge and down the hill. If they slowed down, so did the ball of light. If they sped up, it did the same. They followed it all the way home. When they got within sight of the house, it started moving faster. It just seemed to fly down the street. Right up to the house it went and struck the door with a loud "thud" and disappeared. It looked like it had gone inside. The boys were still about a block away. They hurried to the house and ran in and began asking Grandmaw and the others if they had seen or heard anything. They hadn't, in fact they thought the boys were

101

crazy. The boys explained what had happened and then the whole family looked all over the house. They didn't find anything until they went into the back sitting room. The rocking chair that Grandpaw always sat in, was rocking! No one had been near it!

From that day on, until she died almost 30 years later, Grandmaw said she felt Grandpaw was always near her. In times of trouble or sorrow, she said she could almost feel him pat her hand or touch her shoulder.

I don't know what finally happened to Grandpaw's rocking chair, I know they had it for years. Occasioanally someone would walk into the room and find it rocking. Very slowly and quietly, just as if someone was sitting in it. The family became so used to it, they would laugh and say, "Paw's back." Grandmaw would just smile and say, "He always has been."

THE LIGHTED LANTERN

by Betty Burns Lusher

In the early part of the twentieth century, typhoid fever was common in this area. It was very frightening and many died with it, especially old people and children. Lillian was seven years old and she was sick, very, very sick. She had typhoid. Her mother had called every doctor that would come. Each came and one after another would shake his head and say, "No hope."

One doctor said, "She can't live, but, if by some miracle she does, she will be like a vegetable. She will have no mind. Her fever has been too high, too long." Only one doctor, a relative, Doctor Rowsey, kept coming back. Later he said it was only to see how long it would be before the crepe was on the door.

Days went by and she was no better. Her mother couldn't remember when she had undressed and gone to bed last. Her feet were too swollen to wear her shoes. One evening, just at dusk, she left Lillian's bedside to get a little fresh air. She walked around the house and sat down on the front steps for a few minutes. An old white-haired black man carrying a lantern came down the street. He turned in at her gate and came up the walk to the steps. He said, "Ma'am, could I have a match to light my lantern?"

Lillian's mother hardly had the energy to raise her hand. She said, "Mister, my little girl is sick, so very sick she might die, and I haven't been in bed for days. If you knew how tired I was, you wouldn't ask me to walk all the way around the house to get you a match."

Very quietly he said to her, "I know your daughter is sick, but she will get well. If you knew who I was, you would run to get the match." Then he began to quote Hebrews 13:1-2.

1. Let brotherly love continue.

2. Be not forgetful to entertain strangers; for thereby some have entertained angels unawares.

Before he could finish, the mother was on her feet and around the house. When she came back with the matches, the man was gone. She ran out to the gate and looked up and down the street, but he was nowhere to be seen. Where did he go? Then it came to her - Why did he need a match for his lantern? It was already lit!

That night Lillian was very restless, but near daylight she seemed to sleep. Her mother rested her head on the side of the bed and soon she too was asleep. Some time later, fingers touching her face very lightly woke her. It was Lillian! Her eyes were open and she was trying to say something. Her mother bent close to hear her. In a whisper Lillian said, "I want mustard and bread." Days before, the doctor had said if she woke up and wanted something to eat to give her anything she wanted. He didn't think she ever would. Now Lillian wanted mustard and bread and there wasn't any in the house. Her mother jumped up and ran out of the house and down the street in her bare feet. She ran into the corner grocery and grabbed a loaf of bread and a jar of mustard from the shelf and ran back out without saying a word. The grocer said later that he really thought she had lost her mind with worry.

Lillian lived on mustard and bread for several weeks before she could eat anything else. Each day she gained a little strength. Her long hair had matted so badly, her head had to be shaved. Her back was covered with sores that left big scars across her hips and shoulders. She carries those scars to this day.

Later, when her mother had time to think, she had some questions. Who was the black man? Where did he come from? Where did he go? How did he know Lillian was sick? How did he know she would get well? The mother died in 1968 without ever learning the answers to these questions.

Lillian didn't die nor did she become a vegetable. She will be eighty years old on April 16, 1986. A wonderful woman, loved by her family and friends alike, she is my mother.

Pat McDonald

PAT McDONALD'S STORY

My name is Athie (Pat) Lovejoy McDonald. My parents are Frank and Leonia Lovejoy, from the left hand fork of the Mood River. I am the oldest daughter. My sister's name is Effie Lovejoy White. My mother died when I was four.

My sister and I lived with our grandmother in Lorado. My father lived in Lorado also, with his mother, Louise Lovejoy. My father worked in the coal mine there. My aunt and uncle, Ida and Millard Lovejoy, my father's brother, lived in Lorado also. Uncle Millard was also a miner.

My father married Veronica Courts Smith who had a daughter by a previous marriage, Joan Smith. They then had two boys together, Frankie and Freddie Lovejoy, both are deceased. Then two girls came along, Norma Jean and Karen Kay Lovejoy, both living.

The nine of us lived at Bear Creek, between Salt Rock and West Hamlin. I lived there until I finished high school. My grandmother Louise Lovejor took me back to Lorado to live with my Aunt Ida so I could find a job. I went to Logan General Hospital for nurses training.

I married Lovell H. McDonald before I finished nursing school. We have two boys, Lovell Franklin and David Michael, and two girls, Carolyn Sue and Janet Lynn. We are presently living in Scott Depot.

I spent a lot of time with my step-grandparents, Lafette and Mollie Courts who lived at Bear Creek. My step-mother told me that one day she went to the barn to milk the cows when her granddaughter, Virginia, who lived in Huntington, came running up to the barn. While Grandmother finished milking, Virginia ran ahead of her and went to her bedroom and went behind the door. When Grandmother finished putting up the milk. she came into the bedroom looking for Virginia but she wasn't there. My grandmother later got a message that Virginia had died soon after this.

The summer my step-grandfather was real sick, my sister and I spent the season with my Grandmother Lovejoy, Aunt Lula and Uncle Sherman at Mood River.

While I was out at play one day, I heard beautiful music that seemed to be coming from the sky. I went in to get everyone to come out into the yard so they could hear the music, but no one could hear it except me! When everyone went back into the house, I kept on playing. I could still hear the pretty music. Our grandmother told us the next day that there were lights flashing on and off on my sister's and my pillows. Later on that day we got a message that our step-grandfather had died.

My half-brother was real sick. He was about five and a half years old. He had been in St. Mary's Hospital with whooping cough, double pneumonia and side pleurisy. Back then they would operate to put a tube in your side to drain out the infection. My half-brother had this done and was getting better, so they let him come home. In a day or so, he started vomiting and hemorrhaging from the nose and mouth. Soon afterwards, he died.

My step-mother had a violin hanging on the wall. During my step-brother's sickness, my step-mother heard the violin play several times. My half-brother really liked the violin and would always want to play with it, but she kept it up on the wall. It had belonged to her deceased brother.

I was out in the yard at my step-grandmother's house, which was very close to ours, the evening before our half-brother's death. I heard a chariot and horses up in the sky. It was so loud that it was real to me at the time. I went into the house and then came back outside and I could still hear it. No one heard it but me.

We had a step-uncle, Oscar Disney, who lived with us. He was at a friend's house hunting when he was shot and killed in a hunting accident, just before daybreak.

A day before his accident, I saw fire burning in the air not too far from our house. We lived close to the one room school house. The fire was real close to the school house.

My husband and I moved to Winfield in December of 1971. Our two girls came with us for they were still small. Our two boys stayed in Lebanon. We rented a house until July of 1972, when we bought a house in Scott Depot.

While we rented in Winfield, I had a lot of re-occurring dreams about water and other strange things, all occurring in Lorado where I had grown up. I would dream that I would be on a bridge and couldn't get across, would be in a house and couldn't find my way out, would be at the post office to pick up my mail and couldn't find our box or be at the store and not be able to find my way back home. I would keep dreaming these strange things over and over again. This went on all the month of January.

The Lorado Flood happened in February of 1972. I believe now that I was being warned of the flood. After the flood I never had those dreams again.

THE HAUNTED HOUSE OF SYBENE

by Bill Lusher (Age 13)

When my grandmother and grandfather Burns first got married, they moved into a big house on the Ohio River at Sybene in Lawrence County. It was an old, old house with high ceilings, wide floor boards and a fireplace in every room. They really liked the house and began to fix it up really nice.

One night just after they went to bed, they heard a crash downstairs. It sounded like a china cabinet had turned over, breaking every dish and glass in it. Granddaddy turned on the lights and went downstairs. He looked all over but couldn't find anything that could have caused it.

One day they noticed something else. They ate in the kitchen and didn't use the dining room, so the dining room door was kept closed. But every morning the door was open. Granddaddy said he was sure he closed it, and he made sure he closed it that night. The next morning it was open. He asked Mamaw if she had opened it. She said she hadn't but thought he had.

After a few weeks of this, Granddaddy got disgusted and took the door down and sanded the sides and worked on it until it fit perfectly. That night he closed the door, making sure it latched, and went to bed. He was sure the door would stay closed. The next morning the door was standing wide open. That night Granddaddy got a case knife and jammed it behind the door facing and against the door. Now he was sure it wouldn't open. But the next morning they found the door open.

By this time Grandaddy had had it. He told Mamaw that the door wasn't going to beat him. He went out and cut a pole about the diameter of his wrist. He wedged it between the door and the wall and again the door opened overnight. Granddaddy was mad, but Mamaw told him to calm down. She said, "If that door wants to stay open, let's just leave it open." So they did.

Later that week they had company and were sitting on the porch when they heard music. It sounded like a banjo playing and people singing. They went out in the yard to see if they could tell where it was coming from, but no matter how they tried they couldn't hear it any place except the porch. In the next few weeks they asked every neighbor around if they had heard it or if anyone had had a party, but no one knew a thing about it. One old woman down the road said it might be the ghosts of some black folks that had settled around there after the Civil War. But no one seemed to know anything for certain.

The weeks went by and Mamaw and Granddaddy were about to get used to the crashes, the music and singing, and the open door when something else happened. One night they were sitting in the living room listening to the radio when they heard footsteps upstairs. Granddaddy went up to see what it was but couldn't find anything or anybody. Mamaw said that it could have been just the sounds of an old house cracking and groaning.

The next night it happened again, but this time the footsteps came down the stairs. Now the living room had double doors into the hall where the stairs were, and they could see all the way down the stairs, they didn't see a thing. Well, that was enough for Mamaw. She said she just couldn't live in that house anymore. So they found another house and packed up and moved. That was over fifty-five years ago, and they never did find out what caused all those strange things to happen. My grandmother is eighty-one years old now, and she still wonders if that house was haunted and if so, by whom or what.

THE HAUNTED ROCK

by Betty Burns Lusher

I know a place where the past is more real to me than the present. It is a beautiful, peaceful place. I won't tell you how to get there. I couldn't stand to see the rocks carved and painting and beer cans everywhere. I want it to stay as it is now. I will only say it is in West Virginia. Let me tell you a little about it. First, you must climb the hill. It's a very high hill. Then you must travel out the ridge. At one place there is a spur that bears off to the left. At the junction is a wide, level place. A house stood there many years ago. All that is left are a few foundation stones, one or two rotted logs, and a straggly rose bush. Off to the side is an old apple tree that has almost been choked out by faster growing, taller trees. Most would pass by and never know that once a family lived and loved here.

As you go on out the spur, it becomes more narrow until it is only six to eight feet wide, with the hill dropping off steeply on each side. A little farther on, you realize you are on rock. You have arrived at my favorite place. The rock is almost covered with moss and vines now. A deep layer of old leaves and twigs lies over all but a small portion. Years ago I tried to uncover it, but it's a large rock that straddles the ridge at that point. I finally gave up and decided to let Mother Nature take over and cover it as she wished. For me this is a magic place. I can sit here and travel from the present to the past and back again with a turn of my head.

Looking to the right, you see a long narrow valley going off to the northeast. The hills are covered with trees, and a small stream runs down the valley floor. Off in the distance you can see a house with a garden and fruit trees and some cattle on the hill back of the house. With just a little effort and some imagination, the house becomes a log cabin. Then I dream. I am a hunter coming home with game to feed my family. Or I am a neighbor who lives eight to ten miles away, who makes the trip once to twice a year to visit with my friends. Sometimes I am even an Indian standing tall and proud looking down on the paleface's log house.

This side of the hill is beautiful all times of the year. In the spring Redbud and Dogwood splash the hills with color. Then summer comes, with everything lush and green. In fall, beautiful fall, all the rich colors blend into a tapestry beyond description. Then winter - and snow covers the hills and valley. The trees lift their long black arms to the sky and crack their knuckles in the wind.

Now I turn my head to the left. It is another world. The past is gone. I see a river, a busy highway, a railroad, places of business, a trailer park and houses everywhere. Off in the distance is a roadside park and farther on there is smoke from a factory. It is truly a picture of the modern world, very different from the other side of the hill.

I want to tell you a story about this rock on the ridge. I first heard this story from a very dear little lady who died in 1977 at the age of ninety-three. She had heard it from her mother.

During the Civil War a squad of Confederate soldiers were camped on the east side of the hill at the base of the rock. There was a bit of a level place here and with a little work with pick and shovels, they had enlarged it enough for a comfortable camp. The six men had been left here as lookouts. This was an excellent place to spot anyone or anything that passed up or down the river or the pike that ran beside the river. Once every ten days, one of the men would dress in civilian clothes and travel several miles to the east or about the same distance to a village to the southwest. There was a covered bridge at both villages, and he would leave a coded message under the third plank of the floor of the bridge. While he was there he would get supplies for the next ten days. He had to be very careful because if he were caught out of uniform, he would be captured and hanged as a spy.

112

At first it was a nice place to be. The war was far away and there was no fighting, just long, lazy days in the sun. The soldiers did some hunting, picked berries, played cards, talked and just plain took it easy. The took turns as lookouts on the rock, watching for any troop movement or anything that might look like a blue uniform. The days drifted into weeks and soon the weeks became months. There was a touch of fall in the air. The nights were getting chilly, but fires had to be kept very small. Even though they were camped under the rock, the glare of a fire of any size could be seen quite a distance from this high ridge.

One day the messenger came back with the supplies, and this time he brought something extra, two jugs of moonshine he had gotten from a farmer he had met on the way. The men hadn't seen any "hard stuff" for months and were not long passing the jug around. Naturally, one drink led to another. They built up the fire and roasted some rabbits they had killed that day. They drank some more and as the evening grew cooler, they put more wood on the fire. Someone pulled out a harmonica and began to play. They sang and drank some more. Someone added more wood to the fire, and they drank some more and sang louder. At some point in the evening, the man on lookout joined them and no one took his place.

Along about midnight the party was in full swing. The fire was blazing high and the men were more than a little drunk and singing at the top of their voices. As luck would have it, this was the time a Union patrol would pass, pressing hard to make it to the railroad and the morning train. They saw the glare of the fire while they were still several miles away. When they got closer they heard the singing. They were going to pass by, thinking it was fox hunters. Suddenly, they heard "Dixie" loud and clear. This called for an investigation. The rest is history. Two men were killed and the other four taken prisoner. The rock became a Union outpost for a while. The story around these parts says they abandoned the rock because of strange sounds. It seems that late at night when everything is still, they could hear a harmonica playing softly and men singing "Dixie," then gunshots and silence. To this day there are those who still hear those same sounds.

The lady who told me the story lived in the cabin at the junction of the spur when she was first married. I asked her if she had ever heard anything, since the rock was fairly close to where she had lived. She said she had never heard any singing or any shots, but a few times, way in the night they thought they could hear music far away, like a harmonica playing. She said everyone around called it "the haunted rock".

Could it be true? I don't know. I guess the only way to find out would be to spend the night on the haunted rock and see. But I don't think I will.

"THE LOST LADIES OF SUNRISE"

by Richard Andre

Charleston is a thriving metropolis - its teeming thousands go about the everyday business of life with little time to spare. Modern buildings of chrome and glass reach for the sky as along the highways fleet automobiles dash on their way!

This is the Charleston we know today, and yet a few scant yards from MacCorkle Ave. where the forests edge on the "Sunrise" carriage trail, there is another Charleston, a place of quiet mystery known to but a few. This cool and leafy glade holds a story of long ago - a story of tears and tradegy. An aging memorial stone erected by former Governor William MacCorkle gives us only the bare outline of what really happened there: IN THE SECOND YEAR OF THE CIVIL WAR TWO WOMEN CONVICTED AS SPIES BY DRUMHEAD COURT MARTIAL WERE BROUGHT TO THIS SPOT — SHOT AND HERE BURIED. IN 1905 WHEN BUILDING THIS ROAD TO SUNRISE THEIR REMAINS WERE DISINTERRED AND REBURIED OPPOSITE THIS STONE. W.A.M. (William A. MacCorkle).

Long ago - down the dark corridors of time -long before memory of anyone living today, Charleston was but a sleepy village languishing in the sun. The storm clouds of Civil War were gathering over Richmond and Washington and mighty armies would soon clash in bloody conflict.

Charleston would not escape this national convulsion that put brother against brother and father against son. Some would like to remember the Civil War as a time of romantic adventure full of dashing young men in elegant uniforms. There was some of that, of course, but most of it was terrible misery full of man's inhumanity to man!

Charleston or Kanawha Court House Virginia, as it was sometimes called, lay on banks of the

Great Kanawha River and was thus along the path of the warring armies as they lurched to and fro. The rich lands of Ohio lay to the west and the Confederates very much wanted the salt works at Malden near Charleston. The Union forces recognizing the importance of the Kanawha Valley sent troops up river from Point Pleasant and the first clash was at Scary Creek in Putnam County on July 17, 1861. And although the Confederate forces claimed victory they nevertheless moved out of Charleston on the night of July 24th, 1861. Charleston remained in Federal hands until September 13th, 1862 when Confederate troops swept down from Fayetteville. A brief but hot battle ensued through the village streets and we have the recollection of a local youth Thomas Jeffries to describe it for us, "There came a night when a steady stream of wagons passed down Kanawha Street and crossed Elk River. I followed a crowd of people headed for Coxs Hill as the Federals warned that the town was to be burned and shelled. Someone suggested there should be a white flag hoisted and from some unknown quarter a garment, that ladies used to put on first in the morning and take off last at night, was produced and fastened to the top of a pole that had a martins box on it. We could hear some firing, and another boy and I decided to investigate. We passed through the present Spring Hill cemetery and some distance down the face of the hill and sat down under a tree. The Kanawha Hotel, Bank of Virginia, Brooks store, Methodist Church, a warehouse at the corner of Capitol and Virginia and the Mercer Academy were all on fire. With no wind the black smoke settling made it look like the greater part of the town was on fire. The Federal Army had passed down, but we could still see them both in the field and on Kanawha St. all headed for the old suspension bridge at Lovell St. Behind the main body could be seen stragglers, at times 10 or 12, then smaller groups until finally, one straggled along by himself. The first of the Confederates we saw was a small cannon pulled by a large mule.

They called it a Jackass Battery. While we were watching the little gun, a squad of Confederate skirmishers suddenly appeared coming up the hill. I had on a blue flannel suit and blue cap, and my friend had on a blue coat and cap. When we saw them, we jumped up and thinking we were Federal soldiers they fired at us. Fortunately the bullets cut the leaves over our heads. I lost all interest in things down in the bottom and started up the hill on high, and never stopped until I got in a crowd of women behind the hill! Upon returning to town after the battle I saw several dead Confederates lying on the grass next to us. One body was covered up, and they said his head was shot off. Several Federals were killed in a field near what would now be the eastern corner of Brooks and Washington Sts. One man was killed near the corner of Lee and Broad Sts. He was in the garden eating a tomato."

The rebels stayed six short weeks before returning to the east and Old Virginia. For the remainder of the war the Union forces were in firm control of the Kanawha Valley. The very interesting details of the war in Charleston can be told in another story, but let us return to the tragedy of the ladies. Gov. MacCorkle's autobiography, *The Recollections of 50 Years*, paints this picture: "The road was made up to the head of a hollow, a very isolated place. When excavating for the road, I dug up the remains of two women, one a blonde and the other a brunette. This excited a good deal of controversy as to whom these women might be, and I was unable to find out who had been buried in such an out of the way spot as it then was. I went to my friend, Captain John Slack, who was a Union soldier, a very intelligent man, and who knew more about the history of the Kanawha Valley than any other person. I asked him about it, "Oh yes" he said, "I know all about it. When the Confederate troops were encamped just below your place on the river bank there was in camp two women camp followers, who they suspected of being Union spies. They had a drumhead court-martial, convicted the women and took them out of the camp, up to the head of that hollow and shot them, and there they were buried. This was done by the Confederates . Now Capt. Slack was a Republican, a Union soldier, and honest as he could be, and he believed absolutely that his was a correct statement. Later I saw a friend of mine by the name of James Pauline, and was telling him about it. He was an old resident and a man of high integrity, besides being a Democrat and a Confederate soldier. 'Oh' he said, 'John Slack didn't know what he was talking about. I know the exact facts. The Union Army was encamped on the river bank below your place, and these women were followers of the camp and were suspected of being Confederate spies. The Army had a drumhead court-martial, took these two women up the hollow and shot them and buried them there. I know all about it.' Here was a statement from two men as honest as I ever knew, each of whom believed he was telling the exact truth.

The sequel to the incident was interesting. A man in Lincoln County, who had been a Union soldier, heard about my finding the bones of the women. He died a few years ago and on his death bed told of being one of the squad who executed them and said that it had always been a burden to his mind." Thus ends the MacCorkle account.

Was the awful fate of the two women somehow involved with the battle? We know that the Confederate forces were very active on the south side of the river and so would have been all over the "Sunrise" land. This would tie in with MacCorkles date as the second year of the war but it would not comply with the view that it was the Union troops who carried out the execution. Perhaps there is a clue in the regimental history of the 11 Ohio Volunteer Infantry Regiment: "On the 30th of July 1862, a female bushwacker was captured near Gauley; to guard her Luther Sheets of Company A was detailed. The woman said the initials of her name was M. A. but that she was commonly called Hettie Amanda Jones Atkins. She was a fond lover of whiskey and tobacco, and had a most hearty hatred for the "Yankees."

Could the women have been "bushwackers" or Snipers as we might describe them today? As one might imagine in a conflict such as the Civil War there was considerable guerilla type activity and it was not at all uncommon for civilians to fire on invading troops from behind trees or other cover. For centuries the question has existed; should armed civilians be treated as prisoners of war or villians deserving a quick death? In the heat of battle could two "Tom Boys" have met their fate at the hands of battle hardened veterans?

There is considerable historical evidence that indeed women often served as spies in the Civil War. A 1936 book, "Women of the Confederacy," sets forth several instances: "In giving intelligence to Confederates operating near their homes the women performed a valuable service. Indeed it is asserted that in many cases the success of Confederate military activities was due to knowledge supplied in this manner. Often better acquainted with their own localities than the Confederate scouts and not subject to arrest by the Federals, unless under positive suspicion, many women gained valuable military secrets, which they eagerly communicated to the southern commanders. Of particular note was a Belle Boyd, a 17 year old girl from Martinsburg. This resourceful young lady gained the confidence of Union officers and extracted much information of value to her Confederate friends which she regularly passed through the lines. She escaped death several times after being found out and in one case, while fleeing, bullets pierced her dress. In July, 1962, she was finally captured and sent to Washington, D.C. but surprisingly was released after a month for want of evidence, whereupon she made a triumphal tour of the south! Some of these girls were real firebrands, one Nancy Hart, a Virginia mountaineer, often led Stonewall Jackson's Cavalry on raids upon Federal outposts. The Federals offered a reward for her but as soon as she was captured she secured a gun, shot her guard and escaped on a horse. A few days later she returned with over 200 Confederates and captured her former captors!

In a 1934 book concerning area history, George W. Summers added his contribution to the mystery, in his words: "As far as can be ascertained no living person knows who the women were, although Governor MacCorkle and John Slack are believed to have known and to have suppressed their names to keep from bringing sorrow to the women's families, who, it is understood, now live or did live, in Charleston!"

Mr. Summers was a competent newspaper man with long experience in Charleston and his comment should perhaps not be dismissed out of hand although it is difficult to imagine how in a little town the size of Charleston in 1862 two women of local families could be shot by a military firing squad without someone letting out the story. We must assume if it was a military execution it was not a secret nor was it intended to be.

Two future Presidents were stationed in Charleston during the War - Col. Rutherford B. Hayes of the 23rd Ohio and Lt. Williams McKinley. Col. Hayes left us a rather extensive diary of his service in Charleston as well as letters to and from his wife, but nowhere a mention of the women "spies." This is one of the most puzzling aspects of the case - why is there no detailed account in any known writing either Military or civilian, either at the time or in the works of really fine historians such as Dr. John P. Hale, about the executions? This brings me to a point which I do not advocate but which nonetheless could be true. Were the girls murder victims with perhaps no connection with the Civil War? When the Governor's work crew dug up the remains they would have been buried for about 43 years according to the "Spy" story. It is rather remarkable to believe the Governor could gather so much detail from what must have been mere skeletons. Could John Slack simply have come up with a good "yarn" to please his old friend? I would tend to discount all this simply because history tells us that William MacCorkle was a man of considerable intelligence and astuteness. It is highly unlikely that he would have accepted a bogus story and gone to the trouble to erect a stone at the site. In 1863-64 the Union army maintained a camp called Camp White about where the Exxon facility now stands and that would tie in nicely with the Union execution version but the year is wrong! And although Hayes lived in Camp White there is no mention of the women.

To a historian there is almost nothing so intriguing as an unanswered question, but this may be a case when we will have to simply leave the "Lost Ladies" veiled in the mist of time. I have stood in front of their stone and wondered about them - they were beloved by someone - they had names - they laughed and cried even as you and I, but one day their fate overtook them and they have slept ever since in the little hollow at the foot of "Sunrise" Hill. REST IN PEACE.

Dorothy Nicholas

MY PERSONAL SPOOK
by Dorothy Nicholas

No person enjoys reliving a ghost story either by telling it or writing down the facts. Why tell it? Most people don't believe in the spooky supernatural - unless they have had an up close and personal experience with an unexplainable situation such as I did.

As a child, I lived in a remote little community, and I really had no knowledge of spooks, goblins or ghostly happenings. So, my five-year experience with a child ghost made me a believer.

During the late 1940's my family moved to a town about two hours away from our peaceful country home. Our new house was stately red brick of many gables, which was located in a quiet neighborhood. The house had been built by a family named Woods, for their invalid son. The northeast bedroom, the one that was to be my brother's, had a special built-in bunk bed. There were windows all along the east wall so their son could see the sunrise each morning, and look out on the lawn. He could see from his special bed, the squirrels playing in the big oak trees on the south side. Just opposite of the window was a door which opened on to an upstairs roof. This door was not used as a passage, but only to let in the fresh air and the sunshine. I have described this one room carefully because this is where most of the action to come took place.

This was a huge house, a magnificent house, a perfect house for rearing children. So we first thought! But, I couldn't explain the eerie feeling when I would be playing in the yard; or hearing the sound of footsteps on the staircase at night!

I would awaken in the still of the night. The front door would be open - there would be a pause - then the bottom step would creak. My heart would thump as I would strain my ears to listen. I would pull the covers up tightly around my neck, leaving my ears uncovered so that I could hear anything -

anything! The steps were quiet, but not for long! Another creak -- and another, then up and around the landing came the creaking sound of steps. My heart was pounding so hard as I tried to call for help, but no sound would come out. My only thought at that frantic moment was to get out of this room and run down the hall into my mother's arms before I had to confront whatever it was that was disturbing my blissful sleep. Somehow, I managed to escape the horror by running into my parents' room, landing in my mother's arms, screaming, "Something is coming up the stairs." Mother would comfort me and try to explain that all houses settle and creak. Her calmness comforted me until I had fallen into a peaceful slumber. This was to happen again and again for several years.

At this point, you the reader of my story, will be thinking, "Well all children go through stages, and this is just normal for a child to go through a few sleepless nights and a few nightmares." There were many sleepless nights -- and they were not nightmares, I was fully awake.

A new sequence of things began to happen. My brother and I had made friends with several of the neighborhood children. They had begun telling us about the little boy who had lived in our house not long ago and had died there. Our friends asked us if anyone lived in the bedroom where the little boy died? The one with the wall of windows and the built-in bunk bed? My brother said that the room was his. My brother never had slept in that bed --something bothered him about it. He always slept in another bed in that room.

I knew then, that the spirit of that little boy was coming back into the house, trying to pass by my door and to go to "his" room where the built-in bunk bed was. This little spook was interrupting our life because this was "his" house, that he was never able to enjoy. He wasn't going to let my brother and me enjoy it either!

My brother and I were really not scrappy children, but we always seemed to be into some uncontrollable squabble for no reason. We weren't mad at each other, we didn't want to be fighting. "Something" was always getting us into trouble. Some force that we could not understand.

The creaking of the steps did not end, even after mother had the stairs carpeted. The spats with my brother did not stop as we grew up. The worst part, as the years rolled by, was the awful feeling I had whenever I was in the yard.

Something kept drawing my eyes to the up-stairs bedroom - my brother's room! I could be lying on the grass, looking up into the clouds, when my head would always turn toward that wall of windows. Why am I drawn to those windows? What is it? I would be playing with my friends outside, then in a flash, my eyes would quickly glance upward to the wall of windows. Even when I was swinging on my rope swing which hung from one of the old oak trees, I would feel it. Why did I always have to look up there? Whenever I was in the yard, I felt this way. Something in those bedroom windows tugged at me, pulled my eyes up there, and held them fast. Something up there was watching me! Often, my mother would see me standing there looking and ask me what was wrong, what did I see up there? I would always have the same answer, "I don't know, something just makes me keep looking up there -- I feel like I'm being watched."

It was the case of the vanishing blossoms that comvinced me that the little boy was a spook for real.

My mother had a vase of lovely fresh flowers in the center of the dining room table. It was a large Duncan Phyfe table, with no cloth on it. The chairs were never pushed up to the table when it wasn't in use. It is important at this point, to understand these few facts about the dining room. The vase had about two dozen flowers in it.

As I passed through the house one day, I heard mother talking about the blossoms being gone from the flower arrangement on the table. She couldn't figure out why the stems were there and the blossoms were gone! No one in the house knew either. Then a few days later, she noticed the remaining blossoms had disappeared. The stems and the leaves were intact, but no flower's heads. What was taking place? Well, you can imagine my brother and I had a "royal going over," on that one. But really, we were baffled because we didn't now what was going on. Mother began watching more carefully. And each day she would get more hyper with us because she suspected us but couldn't get a confession out of us. We knew nothing - honestly, we didn't. What we did know, however, was that those blasted flowers were disappearing and we were in hot water over it!

One morning, Fanny, who helped my mother clean house, was working in the living room. She was tugging on the heavy sofa which was against the wall. Fanny shrieked, "La Miz Hogue, comes heer fas them flaurs is heer bhin de Devan!" We all ran from every direction until there was quite a traffic jam of people. We couldn't believe our eyes! There they were! The blossom heads -- in a neat row. One after another along the baseboard. At one end, the blossoms were brown and crisp. As the row went on, they got fresher and fresher. And, to this day, my brother vows he had nothing to do with this. I know I didn't! There was no way any of us could have gotten under the sofa, behind the sofa or moved the sofa. My mother and dad still wondered about what happened up until their deaths a few years ago. No way could my brother or I have pulled off such a neat fashion along the baseboard. Mother never found any evidence of chipmunks or mice anywhere. One fact I know -that is the ghost of that little boy was winning, he was keeping my brother and me in trouble all the time. After all, we were alive, we were enjoying living in the house that was built for him.

Finally, I found a way to live with the situation. This little spook had harrassed my family long enough. The only way to live with a ghost is just to confront him. It was a mind-control situation. Over and over and over again, my brother and I would confront our young ghost by saying, "I know you are there and you can't cause anymore problems. We live here now, you don't! Go away!" My brother gave me a long pointed silver bullet to keep under my pillow. I would go to sleep at night with my fingers curled around it. When I would wake up at night, hearing the front door open, the steps creaking, I would say, "I know that you are trying to scare me again. But, I'm not afraid of you!" Silence would come over the long stairway, and I would fall back to sleep.

The noises at night continued for several years. As time went by, I still felt a presence drawing me to stare upward to the windows every time I was out in the yard. The feeling that "something" was watching me continued.

I was now about fifteen years old. The little spook and I were the same age. That is, if spooks have an age. He was ten when he died -- I was ten when I moved into "his" house.

With great fury one night, a thunderstorm raged outside. Our parents were out of town, so our Aunt Emily was staying with my brother and me. We were having our supper in the kitchen which is directly under my brother's room. We heard what sounded like the ripping of metal and the heavy thud of furniture being dropped on the floor going on at the same time, right above our heads. The three of us ran upstairs, down the long hall, and into my brother's room. There we found a hole knocked in the thick brick wall! The hole was larger than a dinner plate and was next to the bunk bed, the bed that the little boy died in! There was no electrical equipment near that wall. How could this happen? Why did it happen? Would you believe we never heard from our little spook again! Had he given up? Had we won?

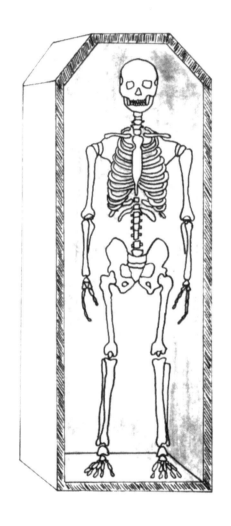

MARTHA CROSS SARGENT
1990

DOROTHY NICHOLAS
PERILS

The perils of a lady trying to live with a skeleton, can create laughter and dilemma. Years ago a friend of mine had a husband who enjoyed practical jokes and poker games with the "Good old boys." One night, my friend awakened to the sound of something heavy being dragged through the downstairs kitchen and down the basement steps. She was sure that it was her husband returning from a poker game. She ran down the stairs and to the top of the basement steps to find her husband dragging a large wooden coffin from the 1800's down the stairs.

"What on earth are you doing?," she asked. He replied, "I won this skeleton in tonight's poker game."

Following him down to the basement, she saw his proudly displayed prize. There it was, a full size human skeleton in a wooden coffin.

"What the heck are you going to do with it?"

"Oh, I thought I'd stand it up here in the bathroom beside this female mannequin." And, he did. In fact, the skeleton stayed in the bathroom for many years. It greeted guests when they would excuse themselves from the gathering to go to the restroom. Quite a conversation piece it was I must say! Also, I might add to this point, people in the field of medical science have practical reasons for having bones lying around. They have no qualms about housing a skeleton either in their closet or bathroom.

I am uninformed as to any unusual events which might have taken place in that house from that night until the fire in the house which took the life of the owner of the skeleton.

My family visited this house many times and my young children were fascinated with "Mr. Bones" as they quickly named it. My friend truly wanted to get rid of "Mr. Bones" but didn't know what was to be done with it. One night two of our children went with their father to get "Mr. Bones" and bring him to our house. One of the children removed the lining of the coffin and relined it with red satin. Mr. Bones went to stand in haunted houses around town and most people loved the effect. But the cold hard facts soon hit me! What do you do with a human skeleton -- I was weary of vacuuming around him and it's difficult to dust a skeleton. I was getting scared driving it to haunted houses via my station wagon. Suppose, just suppose, I would be in an accident - or stopped by a policeman for any number of reasons. What would I do? A neighbor stated flatly, "Bury it." O.K., I agreed, it is wrong to treat human remains this way, going to Halloween haunted houses, looked at by people. So, I decided I wanted it out of my house.

Now, if I bury "Mr. Bones" I would be in big trouble trying to explain what I was doing. How does a lady explain if-God forbid-it would ever be dug up? I thought I would call the police and ask them what would be best. Then as quickly as I had the idea I got rid of it. The police would want a full report -- where I got the skeleton, why I had it, his or her full name, cause of death and date of death. I just couldn't decide how to put Mr. Bones to rest in a respectable way and not get myself in trouble.

Mr. Bones was carried in his antique coffin out of my house and placed in the shed behind the house. After that move, I felt much better.

Who was this Mr. Bones? I had to get him out of my life. The children, as they grew older, grew out of the novelty of him. No more haunted houses for Mr. Bones. No more station wagon jaunts for "Ole Bones" and me.

My husband called the science department of a local university and asked them if he could make a donation of the skeleton. They seemed to be thrilled. So the next step was transportation for Mr. Bones.

We conned our daughter into asking a boy-friend to take her to the university to make a delivery for her parents. Naturally, he was anxious to do so. Not until he arrived at our house did we disclose the mission. We loaded "Ole Bones" for the last time into the old faithful station wagon and they were on their way -- but not until they swore to secrecy, "No Names." We would just let the young scientists and medical students worry with it now. Maybe some young genius will be able to find out who Mr. Bones was and find out his real place that was and will be.

THE ACTRESS

by June Haydon

The whole town knew Murphy Jones killed the Wilson girl. Well, I guess we knew it as well as you can ever be sure about something when you don't actually see it happen. Ever since Murphy came to town and we saw him and the Wilson girl together, we were afraid something bad might happen. Nobody could ever see what she saw in him. She had been the beauty of her high school class, Prom Queen and all that, but some rumors went around that she was 'easy,' if you know what I mean. It was right after graduation that June that she started seeing Murphy.

He wasn't from around our parts and he didn't have our ways and manners. At first he seemed proud that she went out with him, but slowly he changed, and began to look hog tied and surly, while she did all the smiling and making an effort. Evidently the night she died they had a serious falling out.

They spent part of the evening at the local hangout, quarreling. We couldn't help but hear him. He was screaming.

"I don't care. . .you know I'm not going to get married! I told you that from the beginning. If you didn't have any better sense. . .and don't try to shut me up. I don't care who knows it!"

We heard the murmur of her voice for a while and then, "Don't soothe me. . .you knew what you were getting into!"

After he said that, she got up and rushed out of the place. He threw some money on the table and followed her, limping as always. One of Murphy's legs was shorter than the other.

We went ahead and had our usual Saturday night fun and forgot all about them.

The next morning, the paper boy, cutting through the woods to the railroad, found her body. The coroner said she had been strangled. A few days later the news got around that she had been pregnant. The sheriff brought Murphy in for questioning.

Murphy admitted he had been with her the night before. He said he took her home before midnight. He stuck to his story even when the autopsy proved that she'd been dead only for a couple of hours when the paper boy found her. We grilled Murphy for two hours but he denied everything. He even acted surprised when he was told that she was pregnant. So they had to let him go but they warned him not to leave town.

The sheriff said, "I know that no good punk killed that girl but we don't have enough evidence. A quarrel isn't going to stand up in court."

"What a pity she had to get mixed up with that fellow," the deputy said. "She was a beauty if I ever saw one. Gosh, what beautiful red hair." It had never been cut and she wore it straight down her back. It was about the same color as an Irish setter.

We buried the girl and the days passed but the sheriff didn't give up. He had every suspect he could think of brought in for questioning but he had no luck getting any new information out of anybody.

One morning while we were having coffee, he got his bright idea. It didn't sound too smart to us but no one had come up with anything better.

"That Murphy is none too bright," said the sheriff. "Suppose we got someone to impersonate the Wilson girl and come out of the woods some night and say something to Murphy. I bet we could get a confession out of him if he got scared to hell and gone."

The sheriff went over to Abington the next day and talked to the manager of the Barter Theater. Then he talked to some of the actresses who worked there. He found a girl who was shaped like the Wilson girl. She had short black hair but they found a wig in the costume room that would do. The sheriff lent her a picture of the dead girl so the actress could go by it when she put on her makeup.

They talked it over and the actress was a little nervous and reluctant at first. But the sheriff agreed her boyfriend could drive her if he would stay out of sight. He told her that Murphy always walked home that way and she could recognize him by his limp. In case it was unusually dark, they worked out a signal. . .one of the sheriff's men would hoot like an owl three times when he saw Murphy coming. Then he'd hoot three more times and the actress should come out of the woods. The sheriff said he and his men would be hiding across the road with a tape recorder. There would be enough men out there so the actress didn't have anything to worry about. They would nab Murphy the minute he said what they knew he would say. She agreed and they chose a night when Murphy was working the evening shift and would be walking home about ten-thirty.

The night of the plan was cool and dark, but along about nine, a half moon came up and threw a pale silvery light over the woods. I shivered and was sorry I'd agreed to come. Nobody dared talk. We just waited there in silence. I don't know how long we hid but it seemed like a life time. Pretty soon, after I was certain it was time for the sun to come up, here came Murphy, carrying his lunch bucket. The deputy hooted three times and then hooted again.

Just as Murphy reached the woods where the girl's body was found, this apparition literally glided out.

"Murphy," it sighed. "Why did you do it? You didn't have to kill me. I would have given up and gone away. Why did you do it?"

Murphy dropped his lunch box and froze.

The actress was dressed in a whitish, grayish gown, that dragged the ground. Her face was chalk white and the long red wig trailed down her back. She took a step toward him and Murphy backed away.

"No, No! I didn't go do it. Leave me alone!"

She continued to move toward him.

"No, No! I didn't mean to...I didn't mean to kill you!"

With that, Murphy took off running down the road and like one man, we jumped out and chased him. He only got a couple of hundred feet before we caught him.

"You're under arrest, Murphy. You convicted yourself out of your own mouth. That was a trap. We hired someone to impersonate the Wilson girl."

Murphy was too shaken to understand what was said. He went along with the sheriff without saying a word.

When we went back to where we had hidden, the actress wasn't there. We thought she had done an excellent job. We piled into town and headed for the sheriff's office. There was a message to call a number in Abington. After Murphy was locked up, the sheriff made the long distance call.

"Hello, this is Sheriff Morgan. I have word to call this number...What?"

He listened to the voice on the other end of the line for a minute or so, then hung up without another word and turned to us.

"That was the actress. She tried to call me earlier but we had just left to go out to the woods. Her boy friend's car broke down and they couldn't make it. She wanted to know if tomorrow night would do just as well."

The End

Emma Lou Fox

To best understand this story, a little history of the area, into which I am proud to say I have been born and raised, must be reviewed. A little, I say, because this is an area rich in history, not the least of which is the battle that never happened on Sewell Mountain, and the famous encampment of Lee at what we have called Lee's Tree ever since, I guess, Lee tied his horse, Traveler, there after receiving it on this Fayette County mountain. Although the battle that thousands of troops gathered for on Sewell never happened, fighting back and forth between Buster's Knob and Lee's Tree did take place, and many unmarked graves line the hills surrounding what once was Lee's Tree Tavern when I was a young teen.

After the following article appeared in the Meadow River Post, the Rainelle base paper, a resident near Buster's Knob told me that a young drummer boy was still buried somewhere in an unmarked grave in the vicinity of Lee's Tree. Others told me they too have heard what mom heard the night of our seance. And, even though the building is over 3,000 feet high up the West Virginia hill, unexplained sounds carry a long way on those rare still, foggy nights.

The following took place when I was 20 years old and living what is not quite Hines, West Virginia, but not exactly Charmco, either. A place, I would call between the two, but I am sure life-long residents know to which community they belong. This was a ghost I didn't ask to almost bump into.

MEADOW RIVER'S CONSCIENTIOUS GHOST

by Emma Lou Fox

It was one of those damp foggy nights so common to the community running parallel to the murky waters of the Meadow River. I watched as the fog settled like a gray swirling sea into my back yard, the kitchen doorway beamed a rectangle of light, barely penetrating it and mistily illuminating the steep decent to the ground ten feet below.

The narrow beacon from the doorway was the only source of light as I hurried down to the basement to return a forgotten pair of shears. As I came out of the basement door, job accomplished and dusting my hands, and rounded the steps to go back up, I paused. I'm not sure why I did, maybe it was to get my bearings, or check my footing on the first step, but, as I looked up, a silhouette of a young man, slightly built, and of medium height passed between me and the bottom step.

I can only equate what happened next to some comedy plot where the person is hiding in the closet, the other person, who isn't supposed to know anyone is in the closet, goes to the closet, is handed a garment, and then shuts the closet door and is half way across the room when they realize there is someone in their closet. Like the person with the garment, I was up the stairs and in the kitchen before I realized what I had seen. It was very clear; it was walking; and it was not my shadow, although it was a shadow because I could see the steps through it - I was standing still.

After some snooping in the neighborhood, I found out years before a young man who had been doing yard work at the house had tragically and unexplainly died in the neighborhood house fire. Was the silhouette the young man's spirit faithfully returning some forgotten yard tool as I had been? That no snooping revealed. But I did surmise there would be no more trips to the basement on foggy nights.

HARMLESS SEANCE TURNS INTO BIG TROUBLE

by Emma Lou Fox

I had occasion to spend, during my early teens, much time at Lee's Tree Tavern. On this particular evening my Mom was there baby sitting. The baby's sister, two other girls, and myself, besides mom and the baby, were the only people in the building. It had been a long evening, and a house full of girls wasn't what Mom was used to, at all, because of Mom having only one girl and four boys. The baby was going to bed and we had finally hit on something Mom seemed to think harmless enough, at least it would keep us in one place and quiet - a seance! The girls and I went about gathering all the candles we could find, while Mom took the baby and his sister off to get ready for bed upstairs.

I look back on the night now and wonder at our innocence. Conspiritorially, we turned out all the lights and lighted candles. Our mock seriousness was broken only by an occasional giggle. As the oldest sister and I clasped hands across the table, the candle's light flickered and flared between us, making our huddled shadows dance across the room. The younger girl huddled with big eyes in the corner of the booth near her sister. Her wide-eyed exuberance for our undertaking, and the sudden stillness of the room seemed to sober us. We concentrated on the candle light and in, what I hoped was, my most sinister voice I summoned forth a phantom. Neither of us could contain ourselves as we burst into uncontrollable laughter, much to our younger member's exasperation. Only with a vow of seriousness could we convince her to sit still. Again we called on spirits to come from the beyond. A spirit in need of human help. Minutes passed and no sign of anyone, or anything, answering our ghostly request came. We stared into the light of the candle - the swaying motion seemed to lull me. The stillness and semidarkness were comforting, and before I knew it, I was asleep.

I was dreaming of floating on soft fog. I could see a glow in the distance, and I seemed to be floating toward it, although I had no feeling of motion. Periodically the fog would clear enough for me to tell I was closer to the light and above it. Soon the fog seemed to be clearing away faster in front of me, as if I were moving through it faster. The nearer I got, the faster I seemed to go, but I could feel no wind or cold. By this time I knew it was a building; a big building bathed in yellow light that I needed to reach desperately. I was just about to recognize it when a loud piercing scream brought me back to the table and the seance.

My companion was the owner of that scream, and it was evident she was upset. She sat with her hands over her eyes babbling about the candle flame growing. Her younger sibling, who had undoubtly had enough seance for one night, was headed over the back of the booth, her eyes wide now with fright. She had made it about half way across the dining area when Mom reached the bottom of the staircase across from her. From the look on Mom's face I knew I was in for trouble. Being the oldest, I was in charge, while Mom had been upstairs with the little ones. Not only was the youngest of my charge scared to death, her sister was, by this time, in tears. I knew the story would seem inadequate compared to the scene we must have looked. As I related the events of the preceding fifteen minutes, it seemed much longer. I tried to chalk it all up to our over active imaginations, and that seemed to settle that, all the way around. A promise not to continue, one for better behavior, and quite a lot of pleading kept us out of bed early that night. It wasn't until I was congratulating myself on my superior technique at getting us out of that jam, and Mom was on her way back up the stairs, that she asked the question which has haunted me for the last twenty years. She wanted to know who was playing the drum? She had heard rhythmic beating as if someone was beating a drum. The noise seemed to be getting lounder and louder until she heard the scream and came running to see what had caused it. She had forgotten about it in all the excitement. All of us were stunned. Who was playing the drum???

Paul Rowand

CLIP CLOP STORY
by Paul Rowand

When I was a teenage boy, my parents started allowing me to got out at night as long as I came home by 11:00 o'clock. I had never disobeyed them until this night I am going to tell you about. One evening about 9:00 p.m. I went to Kate's Place about a mile from my home, down across the river. This was a restaurant and there were usually lots of teenage age kids there, and it was a good place to make new friends. It was almost halfway between two high schools and girls liked Kate's Place as much as boys. For some reason no one came to Kate's Place that evening, nor later as I found out. I played the Nickelodeon, ate a couple of hot dogs, drank a soft drink and talked to Kate, an older lady who liked all the kids. Before I realized, it was getting late and I had usually caught a ride before 11:00 o'clock to my home with someone I knew and I knew just about everyone.

That night was kind of scary because no one came and I was afraid I would have to walk home. Let me tell you why I was afraid to walk home, especially alone. I was not afraid when I was with someone. This mile was a lonely stretch of road, but that's not too bad, the fact is, about halfway between Kate's Place and my home, there are no homes in either direction for quite some distance. A family of wild cats or some other cat-like creature lived straight up the hill to the top in caves in a rock cliff area that extends around the top of the mountain for several hundred feet. I had heard them screaming, squalling, or otherwise crying like a baby cries on numerous occasions from the porch of my home, and even from that distance, I always had chill bumps up and down my spine.

This would make me seem like I was in Africa or some other wild place, and I would immediately get inside where I could not hear them, and then I would feel safe.

Well, getting back to Kate's Place, where I had

waited until almost midnight for a ride, but there would be no ride that night. So I finally started home, hoping to see some cars on the road, either coming or going, but that was not to be. I liked to see the cars because their lights would allow me to scan both ways. Also, I was OK as long as I could see lights from Kate's Place and a few homes or car lights. To top everything, the night was velvet black, pitch dark, the moon was not shining, and I regretted even the thought of possibly hearing those awful wildcat sounds. What would I do? I didn't have my knife nor my dog, either of which would have made me feel much safer, but still scared. Would they actually attack a helpless boy? I thought they might have if they were hungry enough.

The highway was paved with gravel along each side and the only way I knew I was in the road was by the sound of my heel taps going Clip, Clop, Clip, Clop on the pavement. When I got off the road in the gravel I knew to cut back and this is the way I was walking toward my home. I was approaching the halfway point when I heard a limb or a stick snap up in the hill above and near the sharp curve in the road. I stopped briefly to listen, then I heard this blood-curdling squall in the woods halfway up the hill above me. The hair on my head stood straight up, it could have turned my hair white over night, I was that scared. I started running full speed Clippity Clop, Clippity Clop, Clippity Clopping along. At that moment I knew how it felt to be blind because my eyes were open and big as saucers, but I couldn't see a thing. I was running off the road into the gravel on one side of the road and then again on the other side. I was getting nowhere fast, and to make matters worse, at that moment, I heard something running toward me and it's claws were clicking as it ran on the pavement. I ran as fast as I possibly could, being as scared as I was and I believe I was setting a new world Clippity Clopping speed record. I was zig zagging, running off the side of the road on one side then the other. All of this was in vain because although I ran fast, this thing ran faster. Clickety Click, Clickety Click it was gaining on me fast. I could just imagine being clawed up the back, bitten and killed close to my home by a varmint I couldn't even see. I could hear it so close to me now. I prayed. I prepared to start kicking. I prepared to put up a struggle, swinging my arms, choking, anything, but I never stopped running. Fortunately, this thing kept running past me when it finally caught up. I had never and I mean never, ever, been as scared in my whole life as I was at that very moment. I don't think any fear could ever surpass that fear I felt at that moment, even if I live to be 100 years old. I don't know what it was, but rest assured I thought it was a varmint that just a few moments before had led out a blood-curdling baby crying scream and was about to eat me alive. It could have been a dog. If he had stopped to lick me on the hand, I would have fainted or had a heart attack. My parents would have found me the next morning lying in the highway, gone at 14 years of age, in the fall of 1941.

My parents didn't know why I wouldn't go to Kate's Place much after that night. It was just not worth the risk of a heart attack; in other words, if I didn't have a ride down and back I just wouldn't go!

AN OLD MAN OF THE MOUNTIANS

by Judy P. Byers

My dad has always been "a table hunter." He enjoys the spoils of the hunt, but shies away from actually stalking the game. He and his buddies make a good team. Annually, come mid November, half of them take to the woody hills to seek the deer while the other half wait to prepare the game for the huge feasts that follow. Later, around the table, hunting stories abound.

One season, however, not so long ago, the table was lean, but the storytelling was full of what had happened. The morning air was crisp as the six hunters entered the woods near Elkins. Snow had been predicted. The buddies were eager to begin. They had hunted together since boyhood. Bets were flying on who would bag the first buck. They made the same pact they always made when hunting together. They divided into sub-teams of three. Each hunter would circle out his own way, but meet back at a designated spot by noon. Then all six would meet together at three o'clock.

Bill Kettle, one of the buddies, headed south. He had hunted in these woods before, and his instincts were sharp like the morning frost against his face. As he sat down against a sugar maple to wait and watch, the dark low clouds continued to move in above the bare trees on the hills.

Suddenly, against the gray, he saw a white form move gracefully. His heart quickened. His hand clinched the rifle. Out of the clearing came a big buck, as white as the mist steaming from its nostrils. Albino deer are rare -- rare and beautiful.

He followed the deer as it darted and danced deeper and deeper into the woods. Bill would later say his hunting wits warned him it was foolish to chase the game into an uncharted area, but he was compelled to hunt it anyway.

The gray clouds loomed into the trees now, and snow began to fall. At first, Bill didn't even notice the snow so intent was he on the chase. As the snow increased, Bill could hardly track the white buck against the icy swirl. Soon, he could see nothing at all through the heavy downpour. The white deer was gone. Bill tried to find his way out of the woods, but by now he was completely disoriented in the blizzard.

Noon came and went. The two other hunters met, but Bill never returned. Concerned, the two found the other three and together the five began to search for their missing buddy.

Meanwhile, Bill realized he was lost. Numbness was creeping into his feet and hands and moving up his legs and arms. Fear gripped his heart. Would he ever see his buddies again? He fell to his knees asking God for help.

In the distance through the white, he saw the flickering of a yellow light. It drew closer and closer. An old man with a long white beard and hair wet against his buckskins and coon cap came towards him. A knife and rifle were strapped to his hip, and he carried a bright lantern in his right hand. The snow seemed to part as he walked.

"I was hunting a white buck when the blizzard hit," Bill explained. "Now I'm lost."

The old man nodded with understanding. His calm blue eyes warmed Bill's heart. He took Bill's arm, directing his way. They walked and walked. Bill could see the clearing ahead. He now knew his direction. He shook the old man's hand in gratitude. It was as cold as the surrounding snow.

At the edge of the woods, Bill found his buddies who had formed a search party of forest rangers. The reunion was joyous. None had bagged a buck, but they really didn't care. There'd be another day to hunt, after the snows.

Over hot coffee, Bill told how he had spotted an albino buck, tracked it, became lost, and was saved by an old man of the mountains. The rangers were amazed, for they knew nothing about either buck or old man.

In the spring and throughout the summer Bill returned to the same woods hoping to find the old man again to properly thank him. But, he never did. The thrill of the hunt left Bill after that. He didn't hunt next November. In fact, he has never hunted again. He has become "a table hunter" just like my dad.

WV TURNPIKE STORIES

151

TURNPIKE GHOSTS

by James A. (Abe) Roberts

Until my retirement I was a Sergeant on patrol on the W.Va. Turnpike now I77 and I64 between Charleston and Beckley.

Many stories circulated about strange sights and happenings along this highway. In the many years I patrolled this area I never saw anything strange except for one twenty second interval one night while on patrol.

This night something drew my attention skyward. Whether it was lights or I just happened to look skyward, I just don't know.

I was near Nuckles, or near what was then The Morton Truck Stop now known as the Howard Johnson restaurant about mile 60 on the W. Va. Turnpike. The spot was deep between two hills as it is today.

The object I saw was 1000 feet to 1500 feet high and looked to be 15 to 20 feet across. It was very lit up and sparkled like old time Christmas sparkles at the rear of the U.F.O.

Within 15 seconds it was gone, dazzling lights and all leaving me dumbfounded. I was so anxious to see someone to ask if they had seen what I saw or what I thought I had seen.

Even though I was convinced that I was wide awake and alert. I decided not to mention the incident to anyone. Then when news stories began to appear in the local daily newspaper about U.F.O. sightings down the river (Dunbar) below Charleston. I volunteered to tell that I had also sighted the same objects. Later, a fellow Turnpike patrolman told of seeing the same sight or object.

All witnesses gave almost identical descriptions, like to this day I remember what this object looked like. I don't know what it was but I do know that I have never seen anything before or since that resembled this object.

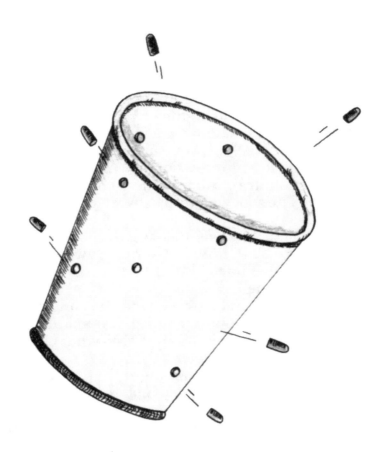

Martha Cross Sargent
1990

154

GHOSTS AT HIGH NOON
by Linda D. Good

Ghostly sights and sounds were part of the surroundings when I was working at the Turnpike Administration Building several years ago. The building was a big, old house converted into use as offices; and, as old houses do, it had the usual creaks and groans which inspire ghost stories on cold, bleak winter days. To add to the atmosphere, there was even a story of the original family house being the scene of a violent murder of a young servant girl and of two men being hung in a nearby underpass for the vicious deed.

I tend to doubt this story, for our ghosts were usually benign, or at the worst, mischevious. I can't imagine a murder victim or the killers, if caught in a time frame of that event, being in a real jovial mood. But perhaps they have a better sense of humor than I do.

Whether true or not, it was chillingly exciting to think of - especially since we didn't have to be there after dark. This wasn't the case for the state troopers as they would check the building at odd hours of the night during their shift. They would report lights being on that had been off at an earlier hour, or noises heard when they were alone in the builidng. One trooper, a real Barney Fife type, told me he went upstairs the night before to investigate the sound of a wastepaper basket being overturned. He stuck out his chest and patted the gun by his side and said he wasn't afraid of anything he couldn't see. As soon as he left, we raced upstairs to look for bullet holes in that poor defenseless wastepaper basket - sad to say, it never had a chance.

Our "Jack" of all trades around the building, once swore he had been picked up by the heels as he was mopping the floor and turned upside down. He looked a funny sight, all covered with water and suds with a sheepish grin on his face as he tried to explain being attacked by a ghost. Could it have been the servant girl who thought he was taking over her job? Jack was a very agile man and it was an odd accident to happen to him. His agility figured in my own direct involvement with the ghost.

Our office was on the first floor of the building and a kitchen was in the basement directly under it. To get to the kitchen we walked out into the hall, opened the heavy door, took two steps, went down more concrete steps to the bottom, then several more steps out to the basement door. There were steps up to the second floor but these were wooden steps and made completely different sounds. There was a rhythm to the sounds going down to the basement - open, pause, tap, tap, tap, pause, tap tap, tap, pause, and then out the basement door. I was standing at the sink fixing lunch and could see at an angle the basement door opening. Jack and some of the guys were playing cards at a table behind me. We heard the heavy door open, taps coming down, pause, more taps. But nothing appeared. The steps had sounded like a woman's and I thought it was my office partner who might have forgotten something. Perhaps five seconds passed, then Jack jumped out of his chair and ran to the basement door. He came back with a sheepish grin plastered on his face and said nothing was there. I thought he was teasing and went to look myself - nothing! The next day, we were again in our positions, with me at the sink and Jack at the table playing cards. Again, we heard the door open, the slight pause, taps on concrete, pause, then more taps down to the bottom. Jack jumped up from his chair at the sound of the opening of the door and by the time the last tap was heard, he was at the basement door. I was right behind him this time - and again, nothing! We just looked at each other with wide eyes. Nothing was there, although we both heard the distinctive footsteps coming down and there was nowhere to go without being seen. That was the last we heard from our noon time ghost and lunch time was never the same again.

The Turnpike is full of ghost stories, mostly at other places along the old 88-mile road. I wonder if it's as interesting since it's been upgraded and renamed. Hope our ghosts weren't too disturbed by all the changes-may they rest in peace.

Martha Cross Sargent
1990

LIGHTS ON THE TURNPIKE

by Clinton Ayers

I worked for the Turnpike Commission at Nuckles, West Virginia, near the Morton Truck stop, as the Maintenance Supervisor. Altough I did not then or now believe in ghosts, a lot of strange things happened that I cannot explain.

On two or three occasions, I heard the sound of a vehicle coming up the railroad tracks. Looking out the window, I saw it leave the railroad tracks, head up a roadway toward the Maintenance building then turn up a road toward the old cemetery. It looked like an old-time military ambulance used during World War I, with an Army insignia. I would go outside with my big spotlight but could never see the ambulance again.

One night with the ground covered with snow, I heard the sound of fox hounds baying on the trail of a fox. Since I loved to listen and see hounds chasing foxes, I took my spotlight and went outside to see the hounds or maybe the fox. The hounds were sounding all around me. My spotlight didn't show even one fox. No tracks of either a fox or the hounds showed in the snow, then or in daylight. I am still mystified by this as I still don't believe in ghosts.

Another unsolved mystery involves a particular window. It would just open or close on its own at anytime, even when you were looking at it! It was hard to understand as it was fairly hard to open or close by hand.

Then there was the mystery of the lights in the building. They would just go off or on of their own accord, without rhyme or reason. The maintenance electrician would check the wiring often but was never able to find a reason for this.

One night, one of our truck drivers drove up to the building when the lights went off, then on and off again. He had heard of this before but after seeing it, swore that he wouldn't stay in the building by himself for a million dollars.

Tales of the off and on lights along with other strange incidents were told at the nearby Morton Truck stop as well as at the head offices near Charleston.

The State Troopers on night patrol had many mysterious experiences. One Trooper told of picking up an illegal hitchhiker. A few minutes later he glanced over to say someting to the hitchhiker and no one was there! There were many reports from turnpike travelers stopping at the old Glass House and reporüng the phantom hitchhiker.

One Trooper told of stopping at our turnpike gas pumps. The pumps were unattended at night. The Trooper used a key to the pumps and was filling the gas tank. No one was around. Suddenly, he felt that two cold hands had grasped the back of his neck. He ran and jumped in the patrol car and took off with the gas nozzle in the tank. The nose pulled off the pumps. This Trooper never again used this pump late at night if no one was around, even if he had to pay for the gas.

There were always stories of the lights along the turnpike by workers and travelers. They ranged from lights hovering over the turnpike to U.F.Os.

BILL TREADWAY STORY

Down Mossey on Rt. 15, June 18, 1986 - 4 P.M. Round disk. Size of No. 2 wash tub. Silver color from behind cloud. When sun touched it - turned over and was gone.

First part of the 80's/last of the 70's. One evening just at dusk, drove my brother up to mouth of Mossey to telephone his wife in Arizona. Parked in front of Ted Gray's store. About 6 bright lights driving at each other. No noise and didn't hit each other. They got behind the timber over about where Plumb Orchard lake is. About the start of winter of that year.

The next one happened in the winter about the same year as above. Saw light moving across the sky through basement window - went outside to watch it. Was moving from east to southwest, erratic motion - till it was behind timber and mountain. Only one I ever saw do that.

Here is a strange one. I am sure it was back in the 70's. Same location up Mossey road as the lights moving at each other. First a round ball - about baseketball size, moved from the east. Copper color, looked like it moved behind something, down came a flag shaped thing that looked like it was going behind something. The lights were colored like neon lights. The flag-like thing had stripes on it. It came down slow then was gone, looked to be about 3 or 4 foot square.

The rest of us are OK as we are older and more contrary. About the same dates as above. Bright light came down in the west, then stopped, then took off northwest same color as the evening star.

Many stories were told of lights on the West Virginia Turnpike. Newspapers carried stories of various sightings. Secret stories were told to me with the persons telling the stories not agreeing to let me use their names.

The sighting included a story of a UFO landing in the paved highway across Paint Creek from the Turnpike at Mossey.

The following list of sightings are from William Treadway who lived near the Mossey exit. Mr. Treadway now lives at Ajo, Arizona.

THE WV TURNPIKE GHOSTS

by Dennis Deitz

When I wrote the book "The Flood and The Blood" I interviewed people who had survived this disastrous flood of 1932. In these interviews I heard of a number of stories of strange happenings and sights along the old WV Turnpike now I-64 and I-77. (From Kanawha River and Beckley, WV.)

When I decided to write "The Greenbrier Ghost" book I gathered these stories for a chapter on the WV Turnpike.

Almost all of these stories seemed to have happened in a period of time from when the Turnpike was being built in 1954 and when it was updated to Interstate standards about 20 years later.

Most of these happenings seemed to have taken place in a fifteen mile section between Mossy Mile Post 60 to the Old Turnpike Mile Post 59. The strange happenings seemed to concentrate heavily in the area of the Morton Truck Stop and the nearby maintenance building for the Turnpike.

This was a natural area for the Turnpike and strange happenings with its long history of death and tragedies.

First were the early mine wars, most of them started on Paint Creek and Cabin Creek. Both are on the old Turnpike, now Interstate 64 and 77.

Both creeks had tragic floods. Cabin Creek in 1916 and Paint Creek in 1932. The floods killed about 150 people. A lot of the personal stoies by survivors are told in the book "The Flood and the Blood" along with pictures.

Both creeks were full of mines and mining towns where hundreds of men were killed by accidents and mine explosions. A lot of murders took place on both creeks.

It seems strange that almost all of the ghost stories I gathered seemed to start with the building of the WV Turnpike in 1954. The Turnpike went for a few miles up Cabin Creek then through a tunnel and followed Paint Creek toward Beckley. Naturally, a lot of old grave yards were disturbed and moved in the building of the road.

Did this disturbance of these graves trigger these strange happenings? Nowhere more were these things than at Morton Truck Stop where a large cemetery had been moved.

It was at this truck stop and restaurant, then called the old Glass House that strange unexplainable happenings took place over a period of 20 years. Many of these stories are not included as a lot of the waiters did not want to be quoted and many were second hand stories.

At the same time a lot of strange happenings took place on the Turnpike and seen by State Policemen who patrolled the highway. These events were reported by these patrolmen especially the ones on night duty. They were reported so matter of factly that someone reading the report would be jolted by the note of mystery invading a rather dull official report.

Why did this seem to stop after 20 years except for a few lights which occasionally continue to appear?

TROOPER SEES STRANGE LIGHTS IN SKY

Excerpt from Charleston Gazette

A state police trooper in Raleigh County thought he was responding to a crank call early Thursday when he received a report of strange lights in the sky near the WV Turnpike. But Trooper John Ferda of the Beckley detachment discovered when he reached the scene in the Sand Branch area that the report was no hoax. Hovering in the sky over the turnpike was a cluster of bright lights.

"It looked like maybe two or three high-beam flashlights close together in a cluster. It was high enough to be above the tree line in the horizon. It was not making any noise," Ferda said.

As Ferda and other police officers at the scene watched, the lights appeared to move from left to right, then dropped out of sight Ferda said he observed the lights for nearly an hour before they disappeared. He and the other policemen went to an area near the WV Turnpike where the lights appeared to be coming from, but they could not find any source for the aerial show.

The lights had no distinct shape and did not appear to be attached to anything. "They were just there," Ferda said. Raliegh County airport officials said no aircraft was reported over the area at the time of the incident, which occurred around 2 a.m.

However, Ferda said he cannot accept the idea that the strange phenomenon may have been caused by extraterrestrial beings. "There's an explanation based in reality," he said.

PREMONITIONS

GOD'S ANSWER

by Maxine Beller

Late one evening about 11:30 p.m., I had a feeling my oldest son, McClure Petry, was in serious trouble. He was a soldier in Vietnam.

Unbeknownst to me, my mother, living across the street from me, and a neighbor, living in the apartment next to me, felt the same way.

All of us, me, my mother and next-door neighbor who we called Granny Burns, got on our knees and prayed for my son.

About one week later, I received a letter from my son, McClure saying, "Mom, thank Ma-Maw for praying for me and especially Granny Burns. I know you pray for me, but this day we were surrounded by the Charlies (Viet Cong) and all at once, they left. I was praying also. I love you, Mom. Rick"

He was nicknamed Rick by his soldier buddies. At the time this occurred, I was Maxine Petry. My son's name, Lewis McClure Petry.

PREMONITIONS

by Madeline Deitz

Premonitions are something you cannot explain but when you experience them you know.

February 1961 was a nice month warm enough to clean up the yard after the colder months. February 13th was such a day. I decided I would pick up the dead debris from the tree in our front yard. As I was doing this, a strong message went through my mind, "Some one is going to Die." I said Lord is it me, my husband Dennis, one of the children, or Mom & Pop, no one in my immediate family was sick. The next morning at 4 A.M. my Pop called me to tell my oldest brother had died unexpectedly.

Another experience I have had is being able to know who was calling before answering the telephone and telling those who were present who it was that was calling.

Rosalie Scott

PREMONITIONS

by Rosalie Scott

I was born on Hainer Branch, November 5, 1923. My grandfather owned the mile long strip; a tributary of the Guyan River. We resided at the four room Jenny Lynn home below the one Grandpa rented; Lewis Dick and Mary Ann (Lucas) Hainer. (The original way of spelling the name was Haner. It was also spelled Hayner, Haynor and Hainer.) Grandpa's home had ten rooms with upstairs and downstairs porches that reached across the front. I loved visiting with them when I was a little girl. They died in the month of October; a year apart, 1931-1932. They were seventy-one and seventy-two. I remember the chimney standing long after the house was gone. It was like a sentinel to me.

My father and mother were Walter (Boss) Frye and Dora Melvina (Pauley) Hainer who died years apart. My pappa on November 25, 1959 and my mother April 2, 1970. She was eighty-one and he was seventy-two. They instilled superstition in my mind that stayed throughout the years. I knew that dreams came true and when I got a strong feeling that I needed to see a loved one and didn't, they died the next day or following week. For example: My mom seemed strange when I visited her the weekend before Easter in 1970. She seemed to want to convey a message to me. The next week, I worried and asked my husband to take me back the following Sunday. He said, "Wait until Easter," which would have been the following Sunday, "and take her some flowers." She had a Cerebral Hemorrhage the evening I wanted to see her and never gained consciousness. I've had many such premonitions in my life and I dream in color. She believed in dreams coming true and I do too. In the way I see it, they certainly do.

She came to me in a dream and said, "You will be a very sick girl but you'll live." Sure enough, I was hospitalized for a body ailment which required surgery but got along O.K.

I dreamt of a tornado in Minnesota and was there in the dream. My son, Bob, always teased me about fearing tornadoes. In the dream, I saw a wheel of arrows in the blue sky with fluffy white clouds. I prayed, "God, please let all my family go to Heaven." The next evening, I received the tragic news of his drowning at Eagle Lake in Crow Wing County, near Brainerd, Minnesota. He had been born at two p.m. on June 10, 1946. He died at two p.m. on August 25, 1974. The Department of Natural Resources sent me pictures of the rescue showing the back of Haverton Furneral Home with a clock pointing to two p.m. I had seen him here in West Virginia the week before his death and cried when he left for Minnesota, feeling I'd never see him again. He was a country entertainer and had learned to play the Trini Lopez guitar by ear. He sang real well, was an imitator and M.C. He played one-night stands in the Northwest and West Virginia. His name was Robert Lee (Bob) Yeager.

Another premonition or dream was the year 1986, when my father came to me in a dream. It seemed to be in a church. He spoke to me and said, "I have something to tell you." I hurried by and replied, "Wait a minute." When I returned in the dream, he was gone. A few weeks later, my niece was killed in an automobile accident on Rt. 60. I heard the sirens and felt it was a relative.

I feel the spirits of the family members departed from this life. They seem near many times. I can be thinking of my son and a familiar song of his will come on the radio or T.V. This has happened often. Call these happenings coincidence if you wish. I know them as premonitions.

171

Bud Burka

OTHER LITTLE INCIDENTS

by Bud Burka

My mother and I always knew it was the other one calling before picking up the telephone and telling anyone around who was calling.

At one time, I worked as a radio announcer in Charleston, West Virginia. One of my interviews was with a physic. After the interview, I took him to my home for dinner. I mentioned my three package per day cigarette habit. He asked if I really wanted to stop. I said, "Of course." He said, "If you want to really stop, I can cause you to never want another cigarette, but you have to mean what you say." I suppose he hypnotized me. I have never wanted another cigarette from that day, November 15, 1968.

I have an ability sometimes to take a personal object carried by someone and by holding it, relate it to something in their lives.

A lady friend of the family was visiting us when it was suggested that she give me an article from her pocketbook to see the results, maybe a cigarette lighter. I took this to another room where it was quiet, held it to my forehead and concentrated for about five minutes. I told her I must have failed, all I could see was this object in a black kettle or pot outside. She laughed and said, "No, you didn't. I was at Elkview watching a group making apple butter outside in a big black kettle. I accidentally dropped this in the kettle."

DREAMS

by Bud Burka

I have had many experiences through the years of dreams, premonitions or things I have never been able to explain.

One of the more memorable was the death of my father-in-law, June 13, 1961, in Palm Springs, California. I woke up one morining at 2:20 E.S.T. crying. I had been dreaming. I woke my wife to tell her I had dreamed of seeing her mother running out in the street screaming for help from police or someone. My father-in-law had had a heart attack. I seemed to have seen the room, color of curtains, the rugs and the furniture. My father-in-law, being a doctor, recognized a heart attack and told his wife to get his portable oxygen, call for help and notify their children that he was dying.

My wife assured me I had had a nightmare and everything was all right. We went to sleep, but the next morning the call came that he had indeed died of a heart attack at 11:20 p.m. P.S.T., or the exact time I had dreamed.

We flew to Palm Springs. When we entered the house, the rooms were exactly as I had described to my wife from my dream. My mother-in-law told of running out in the street screaming for help exactly as I had told my wife.

For a number of years, I had dreams of airplane crashes which seemed to come true. The climax to this was seeing a crash of a plane near Baltimore, Maryland. The plane was blue and white, maybe a 707, with 81 people aboard. I saw the plane crashing December 7, 1968 or 1969, as I remember. I saw everyone killed. Because of past experiences, I made an effort to warn the airlines. My effort ended in total frustration. Naturally, they didn't take my story seriously, saying the numbered flight I had seen was flying from Puerto Rico to New York. It would not be near Baltimore, but out over the Atlantic Ocean.

This plane was not scheduled to go to Baltimore, but due to extremely bad storms over the Atlantic, landed at Baltimore until weather let up. Lightning struck the plane after take-off.

December 7 passed - nothing happened. I was to be wrong. We were watching the television on the 8th of December. The most dramatic news was tragic. A plane had taken off from the Friendship Airport in Baltimore, Maryland. All persons on board had been killed, 79 in all, not 81, but two passengers left the plane in Baltimore. It was the same plane I had seen in my dream. I began to pray that I would never dream of another air crash and I never have.

Belinda Nelson

Renee Nelson

RENEE'S WRECK

by Belinda Nelson

On Saturday, May 12, 1990, I awakened my daughter, Renee, to go to the drug store to pick up some prescriptions for me. I had some difficulty awakening Renee because she had gone to the Scott High School Prom the previous night. I told her I would call her boyfriend, G.W. and ask him to go with her. I called G.W. while Renee showered and got dressed.

When Renee got ready to leave, she asked me if I wanted her to drive her Iroc Z28 or my S-10 Blazer. I told her she should drive her Iroc since it was such a beautiful day. She thought for a moment and told me she had decided to take my Blazer since she felt it was safer.

While Renee and G.W. were out picking up my prescriptions I was doing my regular Saturday chores, cleaning, dusting, and washing clothes. I received a call from Renee telling me she was unable to get my prescription because the store hours had been changed. I told her to come on home and I would get them filled on Monday.

I had just started folding some bath towels and I saw a vision of Renee wrecked. I had a feeling there was something else involved, however I couldn't see anything. I kept seeing my S-10 Blazer wrecked. I tried desparately to see other objects but all I could see was my Blazer. The views or visions I kept seeing were so real I started to cry. I picked up the phone and called G.W.'s parents to see if they had gotten back to their house, they hadn't. Mrs. Mitchell said the kids hadn't had enought time to get back. I told her how worried I was and I was afraid something had happened to them. She assured me she would drive down the road and look for them if it would make me feel better. I hung up! I then saw very vivid flashes of Renee wrecked. I put my shoes on and was ready to walk out the door because I knew I was going to get some bad news. I then decided to call Breedlove's Wrecker

Service. I wanted to know if there had been any wrecks in the area. I had to look up the number because it was in another community and was long distance. While I was frantically looking up the phone number, crying all the while, my husband inquired as to why I was so upset. I told him what I kept seeing. He wanted to know if someone had called and said Renee had wrecked and I told him no. He told me I was crazy and had totally lost my mind. He was so upset with me, he actually left the house. I was then alone, still seeing the flashes. I was beginning to think that perhaps I was going insane.

I found the number and called, Mrs. Breedlove answered the phone. I asked her if there had been a wreck in the area and she asked me why I had called her. I told her my daughter was out on the road and I had a strange feeling that she had wrecked. Mrs. Breedlove said there had been a wreck just down the road from her house but her husband had not mentioned who it had been. She said she would check and call me back if it was indeed my daughter. I was so upset by this time that I couldn't get the flashes to go away at all. I stood with my hand on the phone waiting, yes waiting, because I knew that phone would ring. I felt like my heart was in my temples and it felt like I could feel each beat in my throat as well. It rang just like I knew it would. It was Mrs. Breedlove on the other end telling me not to get upset, it was indeed Renee. She had wrecked within "hearing" distance of the Breedlove Wrecker Service. She had dropped off the road and lost control. She had rolled the Blazer over on its top, upside down, in the river. Renee and G. W. were wearing seatbelts and were able to walk away from the scene with only a few minor injuries. The Blazer was a total loss and the rescue team said the seat belts saved their lives.

The flashes of the wreck stopped as soon as Mrs. Breedlove called to tell me they had wrecked. While I was on my way to the wreck sight I didn't have a single flash. It was over. I knew it was real and my thoughts changed to prayers of faith and good health. I knew my visions had been real and now I asked God for the kids to please be safe.

I later found out my visions started at the same time the wreck had happened. I also was told that Renee was crying for me and she kept calling out, Mommy, Mommy, somebody go get my Mommy. She and I are so close we both think about the same thing frequently. I sincerely feel each time she called out for me, I got a flash of her in trouble.

All my life I have heard of this type of thing happening to other people, but I really didn't believe it would ever happen to me.

Linda Deitz Good & son

MARRIAGE PREMONITIONS
by Linda Deitz Good

We all have hunches or a hopeful guess every now and then. But there are times when another voice is heard inside our heads. I think we should pay attention because it may be a message from "the other side." The other side of what is a moot point. A few times in my life I've heard this "voice" and felt immediate certainty of its validity.

The summer we were 15 years old, my girlfriend and I took a class in summer school. You may think it a dull place for young girls to be spending the lazy, sunny days of summer, until you realize we took a class we felt would appeal to boys (math, history or some such).

There was method in our madness! Wendie discovered one of the boy's father owned the local movie theater and set her cap for him. She would wink at him in class while giving a report, pretending she had something in her eye. Or drop papers just as he happened to be passing by. She was a sly one and well-schooled in the Donna Reed school of flirting. I was observing the reeling in of this poor fish, never doubting she would land him, but wondering how long he would last. She only dated "cars" and this sorry soul had a Volkswagen Van - long, long before vans were fashionable. This van was used for work to pick up popcorn, candy, rolls of tickets, etc. and can you think of anything less romantic? What a come-down from her last car, ...er, boyfriend. Through a mutual friend of both, a date was finally arranged and she was telling me about it on our walk home after school. Without thinking, I interrupted her and blurted out, "You're going to marry him." She replied, "You're out of your box?"; which says a lot for our repartee in those days. I knew from that moment on they would be married; although I would never have entertained the idea for a second without my "voice." Happy to say, I was maid of honor at the wedding three years later. More than twenty years later my husband and I are still good friends with them and are godparents to each other couple's son. Guess they didn't mind my sealing their fate too much.

Speaking of my husband, much to my surprise the "voice" came to me later when I began dating a friend of my girlfriend's steady. About two weeks after we started seeing one another we had a lunch date and when he brought me back to the office I stood at the window watching him cross the street. Once again I heard my "voice" saying, "You're going to marry him!" I was a bit surprised and a little amused - neither one of us asks why I didn't warn him. Ha! I reply, in the immortal words of P.T. Barnum - "Never give a sucker an even break!"

SAVED BY THE VOICE

By Linda Deitz Good

The voice doesn't come to me often, but when it does I listen. By listening to it I was saved from an accident I'm certain would have been serious.

I was driving on the interstate on my way to work one lovely spring morning. Traffic was light with only a large tractor trailer in the next lane about a hundred feet or so in front of me. Just as I noticed it the voice said, very clearly "Slow down". I immediately put my foot on the brake and as I did so, one of the tires came off the truck and bounced in front of my car. It landed in the exact place my car would have been if I hadn't slowed down. The sequence of events happened in such a few seconds that I didn't have time to be scared. Which is totally unlike me - I fall to pieces in emergencies. But even afterwards I wasn't upset, just very calm and grateful. All the rest of the way to work I kept saying, "Thank you, thank you, thank you!"

MEDIUMS

MEDIUMS

In the early 1900's mediums were very prevalent. A lot of prominent people believed in them. As time went on fake mediums were exposed everywhere until every one lost faith in them and almost no one consulted or believed they could act as mediums to talk to the deceased or as they described it "Talk to the Dead."

Yet some unexplained mysteries remained from these mediums. The most puzzling one may be the case of Elizabeth Blake as told by Sam T. Mallison in his book, "Lets Set A Spell."

I remember a few incidents concerning Elizabeth Blake. I some times stayed with my Aunt Rosa O'Dell at Hominey Falls, WV when I was about four years old. A lot of people of Hominey Falls consulted Elizabeth Blake a time or so including my Aunt Rosa. The first time Aunt Rosa went to see her she asked Aunt Rosa why she was there saying you can do the same thing, you have the gift and power, so my Aunt bought the necessary equipment, a horn and a ouija board. She was successful in calling the deceased people for neighbors. She later believed this to be the work of the devil and threw the horn and board over a hill behind her house.

One of the stories I remember is of a neighbor of Aunt Rosa's whose son and daughter drove over a 100 miles one Saturday afternoon to see Mrs. Blake.

They left their father cradling wheat in his field. Arriving at Mrs. Blake's house they asked to speak to a relative. Mrs. Blake said another person wants to talk to you. A voice sounding like their father told them he had dropped dead soon after they had left from a heart attack. They rushed home to find their father who had indeed died from a heart attack in the wheat field.

Years later they refused to discuss the incident.

MARTHA CROSS SERGENT
1990

IF A MAN DIES...

About Elizabeth Blake by Sam T. Mallisan

This story was written and published by Sam T. Mallisan the state auditor of WV in the 1920's. It was published in a booklet called *"Let's Set A Spell."* Mr. Mallisan also published a book *"The Great Wildcatter."*

In the early part of the century mediums were very popular, a lot of people had faith in them. When a lot of fake mediums were exposed people lost faith in them.

My Aunt Rosa, whom I visited a lot, went to see Elizabeth Blake for a reading. When my aunt entered the room, Mrs. Blake asked why she was there saying "You can do this as well as I can." According to the neighbors, Aunt Rosa had this power or gift. Soon after she threw away her horn attributing this strange power to be the work of the devil.

"IF A MAN DIE..."

On a summer day in 1855, and eight-year-old girl skipped lightheartedly along a country road in Cabell County, West Virginia. She was traveling the scant distance from the farm of her parents to the nearby village of Guayandotte for an afternoon visit with her aunt. Guayandotte is now a part of metropolitan Huntington.

Suddenly the child, whose name was Elizabeth Winn, was terror-stricken by the manifestation of some weird force, which she afterward learned partially to control although she never was fully able to understand. Let her relate that story, as she told it many times thereafter:

"It was about three o'clock in the afternoon. Suddenly I heard a noise which came from behind me; it sounded like someone was rapping on a fence with a stick of wood. I turned around and to my surprise, not more than thirty feet from me, stood the spectral figure of my grandfather Morris. It moved towards me; I became frightened. I thought it was a ghost. I ran all the way to Guayandotte. I never turned to look at it again, but I could hear the rapping noise pursuing me for a considerable distance. When I reached my aunt's house, I ran in all out of breath and very excited. It took her some time to quiet me and learn the cause of my fright. When I finished relating my experience, she told me that it was all imagination with me. That night I heard noises around my bed, and my aunt heard them also; then she knew it was not my imagination. My experience became the talk of the neighborhood."

After Elizabeth Winn had been married in her seventeenth year to Zachariah Blake, her name became a legend throughout the area where Ohio, West Virginia and Kentucky touch fingers, and among investigators of psychic phenomena throughout the world. As Elizabeth Blake she gave mediumistic "sittings" for forty-five years at which 150,000 persons saw apparitions and heard voices from an eerie source — voices which more often than not volunteered information known only to the sitters and frequently came up with facts not possessed even by them at the time but which later were verified.

After her marriage to Zach Blake, a jovial, plodding Ohio farmer, Elizabeth lived for the remainder of her life in the tiny village of Bradrick, Ohio, which is just across the Ohio River from Huntington.

For almost half a century the modest and humble Blake homestead was a Mecca which attracted the devout, the curious, the skeptical and the skylarking, as well as dozens of skilled investigators of psychic phenomena. The visitors included governors, supreme court judges, senators, lawyers, doctors, industrialists and theologians. One of West Virginia's governors was a regular weekly visitor over a period of several years. In one year alone — 1905 — there were three hundred ministers of Christian denominations among the throngs which came to the house of the trumpet.

The impressive thing is that most of the visitors came away convinced that Mrs. Blake possessed some supernormal power, and an extremely large number of them became converts to the occult belief that, under certain conditions, life after death is a demonstrable fact of nature.

While it is possible, although unlikely, that Mrs. Blake could have worked a fraud upon all of those who heard the voices in her home, especially in view of her background and environment and the absence of cabinets, curtains, confederates, and other trappings of the trickster, it is beyond credibility that she could have deceived all of the many trained investigators who subjected her to every conceivable test. She cooperated fully in all of the investigations, accepting any and all conditions imposed.

It is not of record, written or otherwise, that any of the experts in the business of exposing fraudulent mediums found any evidence of trickery on the part of Mrs. Blake. On the other hand, some of them made written reports to the effect that the phenomena she produced defied explanation. One of them, Ernest G. Williams, became a zealous convert to spiritism and wrote a book, *The Voice of the Dead,* about Mrs. Blake's psychic powers. Prior to his investigation of the Bradrick medium, he had, after the latterday fashion of Houdini, entertained audiences by producing apparitions, voices, etc., through the process of the skilled magician. A copy of the Williams book, published fifty years ago by the Swan Printing and Stationery Company of Huntington, West Virginia, is in my possession, and I shall quote freely from it in the succeeding chapter of this volume.

At the moment I shall deal entirely with what I heard firsthand about Mrs. Blake from a distinguished West Virginia citizen who, as physician to the medium and her family and also as an avid seeker of truth, was a frequent visitor at the Blake home over a period of more than twenty years. This man was the late Dr. L. V. Guthrie of Huntington, outstanding physician and successful businessman of that city, who was a pioneer in the field of psychiatry.

If ever there was a "man from Missouri," it was Dr. Guthrie. Calculating and meticulous in all phases of his career in medicine, psychiatry, business and banking, he was unwilling to accept as fact anything that deviated from the normal human experience. In short he had to be shown before he believed.

Before he became the Blake family physician, Dr. Guthrie, like all other citizens of the Huntington area, had heard many stories of the strange goings-on in the house at Bradrick. In the beginning these reports, many of which were undoubtedly exaggerated as they passed from mouth to ear, filled him with a mixture of skepticism and abhorrence. He placed no credence in the fantastic tales until some of his professional and business associates, in whose integrity he had the utmost confidence, told him of their own experiences with the medium. Their reports persuaded him to pay a visit to Mrs. Blake. The phenomena during this visit were so awesome, evidential, and fascinating that he needed no more persuasion to return on many occasions. In time he became physician to the medium and members of her family.

In fact it was Dr. Guthrie, in his pursuit of truth, who arranged for the visits to Mrs. Blake of several skilled investigators of psychic phenomena. Indeed, it was he who, hearing of the work being done by Ernest Williams in the exposure of fake mediums, contacted Williams and arranged for the latter's prolonged investigation of Mrs. Blake. Dr. Guthrie accompanied Williams and other investigators on many of their visits to the Blake home and on occasion assisted them in setting up devices calculated to protect against trickery.

Throughout the mid twenties I visited Dr. Guthrie frequently, and although Mrs. Blake had been in her grave for a decade, his hair-raising experiences in her home and elsewhere in her presence were so fresh in his memory that he could not recount them in the most meticulous detail without resort to notes and transcripts of the more important events. He spoke of her with a mixture of respect, wonderment, and awe.

Dr. Guthrie told me about the last words Mrs. Blake ever said to him — words spoken but a few hours before she breathed her last. As the family physician, he was at her bedside. He said she was fully conscious and mentally alert. She interrupted him as he started to advise her, as gently as possible, that she was not long for this world.

"I know my condition," he quoted her as having said in a voice that he afterward remembered as having been unusually strong and clear for one so near the end of earthly existence. "I know that I am going to die very shortly. I am not worried about it because I know where I am going. I am anxious to get there where I can be with Zach and the children who have gone ahead."

Dr. Guthrie said she looked him straight in the eye as she continued: "Doctor, you have not only been our physician, but also our friend. You have seen and heard many strange things in this house, and I know that you have wondered about them. If I were to tell a lie, I certainly wouldn't do it now, and I want to tell you, Doctor, that you never saw nor heard anything in this house that was not real."

Naturally this declaration by a dying woman of great religious devotion made a deep and lasting impression. Mrs. Blake was a devout Methodist, the granddaughter of a minister of that denomination. Since her formal education had been severely limited, she was hardly more than literate, but she was an avid Bible student who was able to discuss the scriptures in an intelligent and interesting manner. It was the appraisal of those who knew her well that she was diligent in all things, fervent in spirit, and a person who accepted the adversities of life serenely and without protest, finding good in all things. Dr. Guthrie regarded her as a very wise and kindly woman.

Mrs. Blake was slender and handsome, and until she was stricken by a crippling affliction in her later years there was about her carriage and manner a quality that observers described as queenly. When she was in her mid-sixties, her features reflected wisdom, maturity, and experience, but not physical age. She always dressed modestly in black, was ever cheerful and discussed spiritual laws with the solemnity of an ascetic. She made no charge for her "sittings," but if a visitor wished to make a contribution he or she was permitted to do so — provided the contribution did not exceed fifty cents! It is obvious that Mrs. Blake's total income from her seances was negligible because she was never possessed of material wealth beyond that necessary to provide the most ordinary creature comforts of life for the family.

Mrs. Blake was born in Proctorville, Ohio, in

1847. When she was but two years old, her parents moved across the Ohio River to Cabell County, West Virginia. She lived there until her marriage to Zach Blake when she moved back across the river to Bradrick.

I have referred to the modest home in Bradrick as the house of the trumpet. This appellation comes from the fact that Mrs. Blake was what the occult world calls a trumpet medium. When "conditions" were favorable, the voices emanated from a tin trumpet, one end of which the sitter held to his ear. As a general rule, Mrs. Blake held the other end to her ear. However, when Dr. Guthrie and other investigators suggested the possibility that she might possess the faculty of speaking through the Eustachian tubes, she confounded and astonished them by placing her end of the trumpet in her lap. Indeed, Dr. Guthrie told me that thereafter he was present on several occasions when the trumpet was not used at all. At those times, he said, the voices came loud and clear out of nowhere and in a spontaneous manner. He recalled one day when the mysterious words from the void were so loud they could be heard outside the house. He told me of another time when, without a trumpet or any other object, Mrs. Blake produced the voice as she rode with him in a buggy. According to him, she did not always seem to know when the phenomena might develop. They might be talking about a subject remote from the occult when she would interrupt and say quietly, "Doctor, there's someone here who wishes to speak."

What, specifically, did Dr. Guthrie hear in the house of the trumpet and elsewhere? It would require a volume to record all the strange events he related to me over the years of our friendship and association. I will select but a few of the more impressive and evidential phenomena.

Fortunately, it is not necessary for me to rely upon memory in recounting the stories that Dr. Guthrie told me because they are included in reports made by him at the time to the American Society for Psychical Research. I have had access to the printed volume of this organization's proceedings which include the Guthrie and other reports on Mrs. Blake. In fact, I have before me photostatic copies of relevant portions of the printed volume, and its from these that I shall quote verbatim.

Dr. Guthrie's report of his first visit to Mrs. Blake is dated May 7, 1906. He wrote of this experience as follows:

Mrs. Blake did not know me the first time I saw her and, as I was dressed with a Prince Albert coat and white tie, she thought I was a minister. I did not give her my name; in fact, neither she nor her husband asked me any questions.

Someone was having a sitting with Mrs. Blake when we called, and we waited in an adjoining room and Mr. Blake entertained us by telling us of his wife's wonderful power, but during the entire wait he did not ask a single question concerning my identity.

When we went into the room with Mrs. Blake, after a few minutes' general conservation, she handed me one end of the trumpet, whereupon it immediately began to feel heavy with a drawing sensation towards my ear, all of which could, of course, have been produced by the medium. I placed one end of the trumpet to my ear and Mrs. Blake did likewise. Immediately a voice said: "How do you do, Lew? I am glad you came to talk with me."

"To whom are you talking?"
"My son, Lew."
Not wishing to give the medium any clue and also not wishing to permit my imagination to get the best of me, I insisted that this name should be repeated. Whereupon the answer came "Lew, Lew," and was easily understood by me, but I pretended not to understand, and Mrs. Blake said, "Perhaps this lady with you

can hear better than you," whereupon my wife placed my end of the trumpet to her ear and said, "Who is speaking?" the answer came "F.A. Guthrie" so plain and distinct that I heard every word although the trumpet was three or four feet from me.

I again took the trumpet and said, "If this is my father speaking, answer the following questions: Date of your death, immediate cause of death, who was present at the death bed?"

"I am not dead but my spirit left my body on the sixteenth day of August, 1904, at 8 o'clock in the morning. The cause was inflammation of the stomach and bowels. My kidneys were also affected. You and mother were at my bed side when I passed over."

All of this was absolutely correct in every respect, but I did not know at the time that his kidneys had given him any trouble but afterwards discovered that three days before his death he had gone to a drug store at Point Pleasant and purchased medicine for his kidneys.

"How long before you passed over did you know you were going?"

"Two days."

This was probably correct, as forty-eight hours before his death he had the first alarming symptoms.

"Why didn't you tell me you were not going to get well?"

"Because I did not want to worry you with it, and I am very sorry that I was compelled to leave my business affairs so badly tangled. Do not worry; everything will turn out all right. There is plenty of property to pay all the debts and leave considerable besides."

(At the time of my father's death his affairs seemed to be in very bad condition — several outstanding notes, several of them necessitating immediate action, and at the time it seemed to me that only by the hardest of work and most careful management I should be able to settle up debts in full. However, this all turned out as the voice had indicated. The voice purporting to be that of my father stated that he was perfectly happy and gave me much information concerning his property, going as far as to place values on different tracts of land.)

"Did you suffer any of the time you passed over?"

"No, not at all." (Probably true.)

Following will be found a brief account of some of my more important sittings.

In settling my father's estate I found a very complicated state of affairs existing between his estate and the estate of one of his brothers, and I was unable to ascertain the exact amount of indebtedness, but after going through a lot of old papers I came to the conclusion that my father owed this brother about $595.00. I asked the voice the follwing question: "How much must I pay D.P.'s heirs?"

"Give them $600.00. That will be all right and should satisfy them." (This would have been his way of settling the account of 595 dollars had he been alive.)

At another time when I had gotten into a law suit over one of my father's tracts of land I remarked to the voice:

"Do you know that Mr. W. is trying to steal one of our tracts of land?"

"Yes, but he can't do it. You will beat him in that matter."

"Am I getting along all right in the law suit that I have against him?"

"Yes, and you should make preparations to compromise the suit. He wants to compromise now."

A short time after this Mr. W. came to my office with his attorney and voluntarily made a proposition to compromise the suit on my terms, which was done. Mr. W. lived in central Ohio and Mrs. B. has never seen or heard of him.

While we were getting ready for this suit and taking depositions I asked the voice if he knew who my attorneys were. He replied: "Yes, Attorney John W. English and Charley Hogg of Point Pleasant." This was correct. I will here remark that Mrs. Blake had no opportunity of knowing these facts and my own family did not know who my attorneys were in the case. One night at a dark circle a voice said:

"How are you, Doc?"

"Who is it speaking?"

"Your uncle George."

"You must be mistaken. I never had an Uncle George."

"You always called me Uncle George. I am your Uncle George Lewis."

"Uncle George, were you white or black when you were on earth?"

"I had a white wife!"

A good many years ago a colored man living at Point Pleasant, where I was raised, had died. I had always called him Uncle George, and it was true that he had a white wife.

Before going to see Mrs. Blake at a recent sitting I wrote out the following questions and have hereto added her answers.

Twenty-two years ago my father took me to Virginia for the purpose of entering me in college. I was an only child and had not been away from home a great deal and was quite young; therefore, he accompanied me to Blacksburg, Virginia, where the school was located, and introduced me to the president of the school and otherwise assisted me in getting started. It was a military school and every newcomer was called a "rat" and it was yelled at him in chorus by the old students until it grated his nerves to a considerable extent. As my father and myself walked up towards the college buildings over the campus the word "rat" was yelled out with depressive distinctness. We went across the campus on beyond the college buildings to a large log and my father gave me some paternal advice. As he was going to leave the next morning I felt very sad and lonely and it was with great effort that I kept back the tears which in spite of my efforts would occasionally trickle down my cheek. At all of this my father laughed and said I would be all right in a few days.

"Do you remember the time you took me off to college?"

"Yes, as distinctly as if it had been yesterday."

"As we walked towards the buildings what was said to me by some of the students?"

"They yelled 'rat' at you."

"How do you spell this word?"

"R - A - T."

"Where did we go after leaving the campus and college buildings?"

"We went to a large grove near the college grounds and sat down on a hickory log."

"What did I do or say while sitting on this log?"

"You cried because I was going to leave you and go home."

All this information was absolutely correct except that part which applied to the hickory log, and in that my memory does not serve me. My father had been in the timber business at one time and was a close observer in all lines that applied to it.

On one occasion a voice supposed to be that of

my grandfather talked with me and I said:
"What caused you to depart from this life?"

"You know perfectly well what caused me to pass away and it is not necessary for you to ask any more such questions."

I answered by stating that I wanted the question answered in order that I could be convinced as to his identity and also to know that he had sufficient consciousness and intelligence to reply.

"The immediate cause of my departure from the earthly sphere was a fracture of the skull."

"How did this happen?"

"By falling down a stairway."

"In what town did this occur and in what house?"

"It occurred in Gallipolis, Ohio, in my son's home."

All of this was correct and had happened about twenty-five years ago. Mrs. Blake could not in all probability have known anything of the occurrence as she had never lived in that section and she had no means of ascertaining anything about the circumstances, especially as this happened so many years ago. Then I asked my grandfather if he remembered what he used to do to entertain me when I was a child and he replied that he remembered it with great distinctness. Then I asked him what it was. His reply was that he had made little boats and put them in a tub of water in the house and that we had played with them. This information was correct and the incidents mentioned took place nearly thirty-five years ago at Point Pleasant, West Virginia.

For some time past I have been endeavoring to think of some method of testing and investigating Mrs. Blake's power that would enable me to form a definite opinion, and last night, August 19, 1906, I had a favorable opportunity. I took eight new O.N.T. thread boxes, all of them identical in appearance, and put different articles in them which had formerly belonged to my father, and carefully packed them in cotton so that it would be impossible to shake the boxes or otherwise determine the contents of them by weight or external appearance. The boxes were carefully packed by me myself, no one else was in the room at the time and no one knew the contents of any of them except myself. After packing them, the lids were placed on and rubber bands applied to hold the lids in position. Then the boxes were thoroughly shuffled or mixed, in order that it should be impossible for me to know the contents of any individual box. After this was done the boxes were stacked on my desk and I requested the bookkeeper, who was called into the room for the purpose, to draw at random one of the boxes from the stack while my back was turned towards the boxes. The bookkeeper did not know the contents of any of the boxes, and did not know the object of the drawing until after the drawing was done and I explained it to her. Then I placed the box in my coat pocket and took my father's pocketbook in another pocket and started for Mrs. Wood's residence where I was to meet Mrs. Blake at 8:00 o'clock P.M.

My wife, L.S. English and Mrs. Humphrey Devereux, who was visiting me, accompanied us in the carriage to the seance. While en route I gave English the pocketbook and remarked to him that we should probably get results with the pocketbook because we all knew about it but that I would bet $5.00 that no one would be able to tell the contents of the box.

The seance opened as usual with the Lord's Prayer, followed by the religious song, "Nearer My God to Thee." The usual manifestiations, table rappings and a few small lights, and the conversation opened up.

There were eight others present at the seance beside ourselves, making it a total of twelve.

The first voice to speak purported to be that of my grandfather and he talked in a loud and distinct voice and said that he had never up to the present time told me much of his present condition and that he wanted to tell me how happy he was and what a grand and joyous home he had on the other side, a home that was not prepared by scientists but by God,.and it was an eternal joy, etc. He talked in this strain for several minutes and gave me some advice which is not important in this connection. Following this conversation some of the deceased relatives of some of the strangers present conversed with them. Later on, different voices conversed with Mrs. Devereux. Mrs. Devereux does not live in this section of the United States and was a total stranger to all present with the exception of our party.

I determined not to ask for my father, but to wait unitl he voluntarily spoke, and had just about begun to think that he was not going to talk when he greeted me by stating that he had not talked earlier as he had given way to the other spirits to talk to their friends. He then spoke to Mrs. Devereux, calling her by her first name. He had known her from infancy although he had not seen her for several years. His voice gained in strength and clearness of enunciation and I thought it a good opportunity to put my test questions, whereupon I said:

"Pa, can you tell me if we have anything with us that had formerly belonged to you?"

"Yes, you have."

"What is it?"

"My pocketbook."

"Who has your pocketbook?"

"L.S. English."

Then he resumed his conversation with Mrs. Devereux and while he was thus conversing I explained to my wife that I had a box in my pocket but did not know the contents of it and asked her to put the question to him. She said, "Judge, can you tell me the contents of the box that Lew has in his pocket?"

"Yes."

Then I said to him, "I am very anxious for you to be able to do this in order to report it to Professor Hyslop and if you say so I will take the lid off of the box and enable you to better see its contents."

He replied that it was not necessary to take off the lid off the box, that he could see the contents as well with the lid as if it were off.

I then said, "Well, what is in the box?"

He replied by saying, "My pass I used to travel with."

Mrs. Blake's control then spoke up and said that his mother's strength was about consumed and the meeting would come to an end, whereupon the voice purporting to be that of a deceased minister pronounced the benediction.

A light was produced and the contents of the box examined and the pass above referred to was found inside the box. I will here state that my father had from ten to a dozen annual passes each year, several of which he never had occasion to use at any time, but the pass found in the box was the one he did ninety percent of all his traveling with.

I have never at any time since I have been attending Mrs. Blake's seances heard as loud and strong voices as I heard last night, and with as little hesitation. One voice, which claimed to be that of Rev. Henderson of Colorado, could have been heard a hundred yards, and he sang a hymn through from the beginning to the end in the same loud and distinct voice.

June 15, 1908. Time, 10:30 A.M. Present, my wife and myself.

Immediately before leaving the West Virginia Asylum (of which Dr. Guthrie was superintendent) I conversed with General Boggs, private secretary to Governor D. by long distance phone, who informed me that Governor D. was going through Huntington on the 1:25 P.M. train and requested me to meet the aforesaid train for the purpose of seeing the Governor.

After a few preliminary remarks with Mrs. Blake a voice addressed me claiming to be Lutie D., the deceased wife of Governor D. and said, "Governor D. is in very critical condition and I want you to tell him for me that he must pray more and prepare himself for the other world and by praying and constant effort he will be able to be in the same sphere with myself when he comes over."

"Mrs. D., when am I going to see the Governor?"

"In two or three days."

"Am I not going to see him today?"

"No, you will not see him today."

Another voice purporting to be that of my grandfather G., speaks and after some commonplace remarks I asked, "Grandpa, can you tell me what is the matter with Aunt Salina?"

"Yes, your Aunt Salina is in very critical condition, will live only a short time and if you should ask her what is the matter she would say ulceration of the stomach but she has cancer of the stomach."

Mrs. Blake does not know who Aunt Salina is or where she lives or anything about her.

In this connection I will state that Aunt Salina died five days after this and when I attended

203

the funeral at Gallipolis, Ohio, I asked her daughter what Aunt Salina seemed to think her trouble was and she told me that she invariably referred to her trouble as being sores in her stomach and never referred to it as cancer. This was entirely unknown to me although I was aware of the fact that she had a cancer of the stomach but am positively certain that Mrs. Blake knew nothing of any of these facts.

Another voice addressed me claiming to be that of my father and after some conversation which was not particularly evidential, said, "Lew, I told you twelve months ago that your mother was in a very critical condition. You now realize that what I then told you was correct. She will not live very long. The operation which you had performed was only a temporary benefit and do not operate on her anymore, as nothing will do her any good."

In this connection I wish to state that a year ago my mother's health was apparently better than it had been for several years, and we had no reason to have any apprehension as to her condition but the voice purporting to be my father's told me then that her condition was deceptive and that her health was very bad. About ten months ago she began to show symptons of a malignant growth which has steadily progressed until now. She is practically bedfast all the time. The above referred to operation was performed with a view to temporary relief and it is possible that Mrs. Blake knew something of the particulars. However, Mrs. Blake had no normal means of knowing more than my mother's condition twelve months ago that I knew myself and it is quite evident that the malignant growth had developed a year ago but had not sufficiently advanced to produce symptoms. I hurried through my sitting with Mrs. Blake in order to go back to the West Virginia

Asylum, eat my dinner and meet the 1:25 train. As I drove up to the front porch of the Asylum I was informed that General Boggs had tried to get me by long distance phone twice during my absence and on the second unsuccessful effort he told the bookkeeper to leave word for me that the Governor was not in condition to travel and consequently would not be on the 1:25 train, but would probably be able to take the trip in two or three days. This confirmed the above information. However, on the 17th the Governor was able to make the trip and I accompanied him as far as Cincinnati.

This experienced strengthened the doctor's confidence in Mrs. Blake's integrity. However, despite that confidence it was evident from my many conversations with him that there still lurked in the recesses of his very practical mind a shrunken shred of skepticism. Certainly, he admitted, the evidence was overwhelming, and he further conceded that every other theory by which he sought to rationalize the phenomena led him up a blind alley. Yet he still wondered, as countless millions of others who have pondered the cosmic riddle: "If a man die, shall he live again?"

It would seem to me that until psychic research and psychiatry have extended their horizons, positive answers to the phenomena produced by Mrs. Blake and others must remain shrouded in the same cloud of occult speculation that has enveloped similar thaumaturgy through the ages. Because of their very nature these supernormal manifestations cannot be measured by the slide rule of mathematics. But it certainly is obvious that there are other forces in the universe than those that are mechanical.

The question involved in the occult phenomena strikes me as not so much one of the survival of personality as whether there can be communication between the two worlds. Man has been aware for centuries that there are forces and objects about him that cannot be apprehended by his physical senses. Albert Pike phrased it aptly and beautifully when he wrote:

"A dim consciousness of infinite mystery and grandeur lies beneath all the commonplace of life. There is an awfulness and a majesty around us, in all our little worldliness. The rude peasant from the Apennines, asleep at the foot of a pillar in a majestic Roman church, seems not to hear or see, but to dream only of the herd he feeds or the ground he tills in the mountains. But the choral symphonies fall softly upon his ear, and the gilded arches are dimly seen through his half-slumbering eyelids."

If death is but an incident in the continuity of life, then that would seem to be the most stupendous fact of nature, and one which would excite the interest and investigation of all profound thinkers. Strangely enough, it has been my observation that events which defy explanation by any known laws of physics arouse only superficial interest. Most people are inclined to shrug off such phenomena, no matter how well documented, by ascribing them to coincidence, overwrought imagination, or downright fraud. Others accept them as factual occurrences but airly dismiss them as "just one of those things." Thus, to cite but a single instance, they recognize that Joan of Arc was guided by the voices, but they do not seriously speculate upon the source and identity of those voices.

Perhaps it is only natural that men should instinctively shrink from exploration on the unknown, and if they are devout Christians, prefer to rely upon faith in other worlds after this. Undoubtedly the fear of what may lurk behind the veil acts as deterrent to investigation, but it could well be that it is something inherent in a man's nature that checks the impulse to seek certain personal knowledge of the survival of personality after death. In other words, if communication between the two worlds is possible and under certain conditions, it is still unnatural, unwholesome, and perhaps dangerous practice.

Bulwer Lytton may have spoken from a mountain top of wisdom when he wrote, a century ago, that through modifications of matter nature mercifully screens us from the unseen world.

It must be apparent to even the most rudimentary student of physics that the countless different forms of matter, from the coarsest field stone to such evanescent things as electricity are differentiated by the law of motion and number, or, more simply stated, by the density of particle and the rate of vibration. One wonders about the other forces, objects, forms, and colors that may and undoubtedly do exist all about and around us but which we cannot perceive within the range of our senses.

It seems reasonable to assume that a man is progressively made aware of some of these other forces as he acquires the wisdom to use them constructively. Such a hypothesis would rationalize the instinctive disinclination of man, in his present position in the evolutionary scale, to delve deeply into the supernormal.

NOTES

The students in English 372, Folk Literature, Fall Semester 1990, Clarksburg Campus of Fairmont State College were directd by their professor, Dr. Judy P. Byers, to motif and to identify tale typing for the collecion. Each contribution is documented by the student's name appearing in paranthesis at the end of each note.

"The True Story of the Greenbrier Ghost"
    Secondary Informant: Dennis Deitz
"A Greenbrier Ghost Story"
    Secondary Informant: George Deitz Collection
    Tale Type: Revengeful Ghost
    Motifs: E231, return from dead to reveal murder; E231.1, ghost tells name of murderer; E221, dead spouse's malevolent return; E224, dead child's friendly return to parent; E413, murdered person cannot rest in grave; E421.1.1, ghost visible to one person alone; E411.10, person who dies violent death cannot rest in grave; E402.1.1, vocal sound of ghost of human being
                                        (Terry L. Spencer)
"The Unlawful Baptism of Edward Shue"
    Primary Informant; G. S. McKeever
    Tale Type: This is not a ghost tale, but an interesting personal narrative that sheds more light on the fiendish character of Edward Shue in "The Greenbrier Ghost." Another variant of the tale was collected by Dr. Ruth Ann Musick and appears in **Coffin Hollow and Other Ghost Tales** (pp. 15-19) as "The Shue Mystery." The informant was Eleanor harper.
                                        (Judith A. Lively)
"The Ghost of Shelton College"
    Primary Informant: Janet Quillen who had the encounter as a child growing up
    Tale Type: Poltergeist - a pinkish lady sighted in haunted house
    Motif: E421.3 Luminous ghosts
                                        (Allene Baker)

"A Ghost in the House"
Secondary Informant: Jessie Patterson and
Amanda   Holstein
Tale Type: Poltergeist
Motif: E421.3 Luminous ghosts
(Allene Baker)

"The Old Haunted House"
Secondary Informant: Judith A. Gross
Tale Type: Poltergeist
Motifs: E402, mysterious ghostlike noises
heard; E402.1.2, foot steps of invisible ghost heard;
E281, ghost haunts house; E587, ghosts walk at
certain times
(John Nesbitt)

"Bicycle Wreck"
Primary Informant: Jason Hill, age 10
Tale Type: Dream premonition story from a
child
Motifs: F900, extraordinary occurrences; F647,
marvelous sensitiveness
(Crystal Verettozzi)

"Our Friends"
Primary Informant: M. E. Huber
Tale Type: Poltergeist (three ghosts: our friend,
a dog, and a cat)
Motifs: E281, ghost haunts house; E544, ghost
leaves evidence of appearance; E321.3, ghost
haunts particular room, E599.10, playful
revenant; E402, mysterious ghostlike noises
heard; E423, revenant in animal form; E521.2,
ghost of a dog; E521.3, ghost of a cat; E421.1,
invisible ghost; E402.12, footsteps of invisible
ghost heard
(Phyllis Jean Wilson-Moore)

"The Don Page Family and Their Fun Loving
House Ghost/Guest Homer"
Primary Informant: Don Page
Tale Type: Poltergeist
Motifs: E421.1, invisible ghost; E281, ghost
haunts house; E402.1.8, miscellaneous sounds
made by ghost of human being; E544, ghost leaves

evidence of his appearance; E599.10, playful revenant; E402.1.2, footsteps of invisible ghost heard; E402, mysterious ghostlike noises heard

(Terry L. Spencer)

"Jerry's Vision and Other Strange Events"
Secondary Informant: Opal Haynes Anderson
Tale Type: Group of strange encounters ranging from poltergeists, to a witch tale, to a devil tale to even signs and tokens of impending disaster.
Motif: Z11, Endless tales

(Judith A. Lively)

"James Godfrey Story"
Primary Informant: James Godfrey
Tale Type: Poltergeist
Motifs: E421.3, luminous ghosts; E281, ghost haunts house

(Judith A. Lively)

"April Dawn Persinger's Story"
Primary Informant: April Dawn Persinger, age 11
Tale Type: Two poltergeist stories
Motifs: E440, walking ghost "laid" (the little girl ghost); E215, the dead rider (the car)

(Dianne S. Stewart)

"The Ashton Ghost"
Secondary Informant: Joyce Moore and Martha Cross Sargent
Tale Type: Revengeful ghost (returns to seek justice; similar to "The Greenbrier Ghost")
Motifs: E421.3, luminous ghost; E421.1.1, ghost visible to one person alone, E402.1.1, vocal sounds of ghost of human being; E587, ghost walks at certain times; E402.1.8, miscellaneous sounds made by ghost of human being. Ghost bound to earth because of unresolved circumstances in life.

(Terry L. Spencer)

"Grandma's Story"
Secondary Informant: Kevin P. Anderson
Tale Type: Four encounters: revengeful ghosts and poltergeist ghosts with one encounter being a

UFO siting in 1970s
Motifs: E421.1.1, ghost visible to one person alone; E402, mysterious ghostlike noises; E440, walking ghost "laid"; E232.1, return from dead to slay own murderer; E281, ghost haunts house; E422.1.3, wandering ghost makes attack; F900, extraordinary occurrences.
(Sandi Palmer)

"Ghosts at Brigadoon"
Primary Informant: Bob Jacobus
Tale Type: Poltergeist. A primary encounter by a man of the ministry who links ghosts with angels and demons. His story is presented like a sermon.
Motifs: E430, defense against ghost; E756.1, devils and angels contest for man's soul
(Chris Dotson)

'The Ghostly Couch"
Primary Informant: Margaret Elswick, as experienced by her and her friends and relatives.
Tale Type: Poltergeist
Motifs: E413, murdered person cannot rest in grave; E440, walking ghost "laid".

"The Lady Who Loved Cats"
Primary Informant: Margaret Elswick
Tale Type: Benevolent ghost (a cat)
Motifs: D702.1.1, cat's paw cut off: woman's hand missing; E361, return from dead to stop weeping; E423, revenant in animal form; E440, walking ghost "laid"
(Erin Arnett)

"The Mystery Weeping Willow Tree"
Secondary Informant: Margaret Elswick
Tale Type: Poltergeist
Motifs: E410, the unquiet grave; E413, murdered person cannot rest in grave; E440, walking ghost "laid"; E631, reincarnation in plant growing from grave
(Heidi Earnest)

"Sisters A'Riding"
    Secondary Informant: June Haydon
    Tale Type: Poltergeist
    Motifs: E215, the dead rider; E414, drowned person cannot rest in peace
                        (Janie Steele)

"Poppie's Ghost"
    Primary Informant: Rosalie Scott
    Tale Type: Benevolent ghost
    Motif: E352, dead returns to restore stolen goods
                        (Chris Dotson)

"Connie and the Ouija Board"
    Secondary Informant: Margaret (Peggy) Miller
    Tale Type: Two stories: (a) The first is not a ghost tale but an unusual account of an object serving as a medium to link the dead with the living. The Ouija Board is a messenger or oracle.
    Motifs: D800, magic objects; D1700, magic powers. (b) The second story is a supernatural helper in which magically help comes (in the form of a stranger) to aid character in distress. Indication that the help is supernatural, angelical; D1700, magic powers
                        (Erin Arnett)

"The Blue Light"
    Primary Informant: Carol McClung, as experienced by her and her co-workers
    Tale Type: A premonition of death often seen in hospitals
    Motif: M340, unfavorable prophecy, a variation
                        (Barbara Wolfe)

"A Ball of Light"
    Secondary Informant: Betty Burns Lusher, as happened to her family members.
    Tale Type: Poltergeist
    Motifs: E421.3, luminous ghosts; E710, external soul; E761, like token
                        (Barbara Wolfe)

212

"The Lighted Lantern"
    Secondary Informant: Betty Burns Lusher
    Tale Type: Supernatural helper (indicated that
the helpful stranger was an angel)
    Motifs: N2.2, lives wagered; F900, extra-
ordinary occurrences
                                    (Heidi Earnest)

"Pat McDonald's Story"
    Primary Informant: Athie (Pat) Lovejoy
McDonald
    Tale Type: There are really five premonition
narratives, four of which were actually experienced by the informant. The premonitions were
intriguing signs of impending death or disaster,
such as beautiful music from the sky; sound of loud
chariots and horses riding through the sky; signs
of fire burning in the sky; and many reoccurring
dreams about water and being lost.
                                    (Chris Dotson)

"The Haunted House of Sybene"
    Secondary Informant: Bill Lusher, age 13
    Tale Type: Poltergeist
    Motifs: E238, dinner with the dead; E410,
unquiet dead; E493, dead men dance; F601,
extraordinary companions
                                    (Crystal Verettozzi)

"The Haunted Rock"
    Secondary Informant: Betty Burns Lusher,
slain confederate soldiers "relive" events of their
deaths; harmonica playing "Dixie", shots then
silence
    Tale Type: Poltergeist, restless spirits
    Motifs: E413, murdered persons cannot rest in
graves; E410, the unquiet graves; E402, mysterious
ghostlike noises heard; E275, ghosts haunt place
of great accident or misfortune; E337, ghosts
reenact scene from own lifetimes
                                    (Charlotte Wright)

"The Lost Ladies of Surise"
    Secondary Informant: Richard Andre recounts
historical events

213

Tale Type: Not a ghost tale; a narrative of events that occurred in or near Charleston, WV, during the Civil War. Includes materials from diaries, folklore, and from a biography. There is a mystery included in this piece which involves the lost ladies.

(Phyllis Jean Wilson-Moore)

"My Personal Spook"
Primary Informant: Dorothy Nicholas, Child's spirit haunts his home that he died in at age 10.
Tale Type: Poltergeist, restless spirit
Motifs: E410, the unquiet grave; E402, ghostlike noises heard; E281, ghost haunts house

(Charlotte Wright)

"Dorothy Nicholas Perils"
Primary Informant: Dorothy Nicholas
Tale Type: This is not really a ghost tale, but a narrative about the laughter and dilemma of living with a skeleton in the house.

(Janie Steele)

"The Actress"
Primary Informant: June Haydon
Tale Type: Revengeful ghost
Motifs: E231.5, ghost returns to murderer and causes him to confess

"Meadow River's Conscientious Ghost"
Primary Informant: Emma Lou Fox
Tale Type: Poltergeist (Shadow Ghost)
Motifs: E411.10, persons who die violent or accidental deaths cannot rest in grave; E275, ghost haunts place of great accident or misfortune; E281.3, ghost haunts particular room in house; E281, ghost haunts house; E421.4, ghost as shadow

(John Nesbitt)

"Harmless Seance Turns Into Big Trouble"
Primary Informant: Emma Lou Fox
Tale Type: Variation of Poltergeist
Motif: E440, walking ghost "laid"

"Clip Clop Story"
    Primary Informant: Paul Rowand
    Tale Type: Not really a ghost tale, but a variant of a suspenseful encounter with perhaps a wild cat
    Motifs: B720, fanciful physical qualities of animals; E423, revenant in animal form
                         (Allene Baker)

"An Old Man of the Mountains"
    Secondary Informant: Judy P. Byers as told to her by   her father Alexander Prozzillo
    Tale Type: Supernatural helper in which magically help comes (in the form of a stranger) to aid character in distress. Indication that the help is supernatural, angelical
    Motif: D1700, magic powers
                         (Judy P. Byers)

"Trooper Sees Strange Things"
    Primary Informant: Trooper Steffick
    Tale Type: Poltergeist (haunted highways - strange white cow)
    Motifs: E423, revenant in animal form; Z12, unfinished tales. Ghost appears to more than one person
                         (Judith A. Lively)

"Turnpike Ghosts"
    Primary Informant: James A. (Abe) Roberts
    Tale Type: Polgergeist (variant of Hitchhiking Ghost)
    Motif: F900, extraordinary occurrences
                         (Dianne S. Stewart)

"Ghosts at High Noon"
    Primary Informant: Linda D. Good
    Tale Type: Poltergeist
    Motifs: E275, ghost haunts place of great misfortune or accident; E334, non-malevolent ghost haunts scene of former misfortune, crime, or tragedy; E281, ghost haunts house; E544, ghost leaves evidence of appearance; E293, ghost frightens people; E599.10, playful revenant;

E402.18, miscellaneous sounds made by ghost of human being; E421.1, invisible ghosts; E402.12, footsteps of invisible ghost heard

    (Phyllis Jean Wilson-Moore)

"Lights on the Turnpike"
 Primary Informant: Clinton Ayers
 Tale Type: Lights go on and off at a maintenance building, cold hands on trooper's neck while he started to pump gas, disappearing hitchhiker; poltergeists and restless spirit
 Motifs: E422.1.3, ghost with ice cold hands; E402, ghostlike noises

    (Charlotte Wright)

"Bill Treadway Story"
 Primary Informant: William Treadway
 Tale Type: Poltergeist
 Motif: F900, extraordinary circumstances

    (Sandi Palmer)

"The WV Turnpike Ghost"
 Secondary Informant: Dennis Deitz
 Tale Type: Poltergeist (variations)
 Motifs: F900, extraordinary occurrences; E410, the unquiet grave; E413, murdered person cannot rest in grave; E440, walking ghost "laid"; E414, drowned person cannot rest in peace

    (Heidi Earnest)

"Trooper Sees Strange Lights In Sky"
 Exerpt from **Charleston Gazette**
 Tale Type: Poltergeist
 Motifs: F900, extraordinary occurrences; E440, walking ghost "laid"

    (Yvonne Robertson)

"God's Answer"
 Primary Informant: Maxine Beller
 Tale Type: Premonition of soldier son being in trouble in Vietnam sending message for mother to pray (a feeling)

    (Janie Steele)

"Premonitions"
  Primary Informant: Madeline Deitz
  Tale Type: Premonitions (Mrs. Deitz's account doesn't involve murder but other details are similar)
  Motifs: D1810.8.3.1, warning in dream fulfilled; D1810.8.2.3, murder made known in dream
                    (Nicole Molnar)

"Other Little Incidents"
  Primary Informant: Bud Burka
  Tale Type: Premonitions
  Motifs: First tale M or D700, person disenchanted, ordaining the future. Second tale D1611, magic object answers for fugitive; D1811, thumb of knowledge or F647, marvelous sensitiveness
                    (Dianne S. Stewart)

"Dreams"
  Primary Informant: Bud Burka
  Tale Type: Premonitions (psychic)
  Motifs: D1810.8.3.1, warning in dream fulfilled; 720 (cumulative tales)
                    (Nicole Molnar)

"Renee's Wreck"
  Primary Informant: Belinda Nelson
  Tale Type: Premonition (forewarning)
  Motif: M340, unfavorable prophecy
                    (Yvonne Robertson)

"Marriage Premonitions"
  Primary Informant: Linda Deitz Good
  Tale Type: Premonition (a feeling, inner voice)
  Motif: H310, suitor tests
                    (Crystal Verettozzi)

"Saved by the Voice"
  Primary Informant: Linda Deitz Good
  Tale Type: Premonition (feeling, inner voice)
  Motif: M340, unfavorable prophecy, variant
                    (John Nesbitt)

"Mediums"
    Tale Type: Medium (a person through whom commuications are supposedly sent to the living from spirits of the dead)
                        (Erin Arnett)

"If a Man Dies"
    Secondary Informant: About Elizabeth Blake by   Sam T. Mallison
    Tale Type: Medium
    Motifs: E364, dead returns to say farewell; 720, cumulative tales
                        (Nicole Molnar)